THE PUPPET MAKER'S BONES

ALISA TANGREDI

The Puppet Maker's Bones
Copyright ©2012 by Alisa Tangredi
All rights reserved.

First Print Edition, Createspace April 2012

This is a work of fiction. Apart from actual historical people, events, and locales that figure in the narrative, all names, characters, places, and incidents are the products of the author's imagination or are used fictitiously. Any resemblance to current events or locales, or to living persons, is entirely coincidental.

This book is protected under the copyright laws of the United States of America. Any reproduction or other unauthorized use of the material or artwork herein is prohibited.

Cover design by Flipcity Books
flipcitybooks.com

Formatted by CyberWitch Press
cyberwitchpress.com

*This book is dedicated to my husband,
the handsome man who saves me from my monsters.*

And yearning, weaned away these many years,
Grips me for that grave quiet world of ghosts;
My verse waits on the undecided airs
And like a wind harp sways and sounds and rests;
Cold visitation and a rush of tears,
Hardly at all the strict heart still resists,
What I possess looks far away to me,
Things vanished are becoming my reality

> *Johann Wolfgang von Goethe,*
> *Faust: The First Part of the Tragedy*

Chapter 1

Present Day: Pasadena, California

Mr. Pavel Trusnik pulled on the custom blackout curtains that covered the living room window, ensuring passersby could not sneak a glimpse into his home. The drapes enabled him to look out, but no one could look in. How many years had he paid attention to the mundane ritual of ensuring the drapes were closed? When had he last ventured out the front door? Perhaps in 1942? The neighbor boys had batted a ball through the window. A painful memory of that morning tugged at him. During one of the wars perhaps, but if so, which one? He could not say, for there'd been too many to track. His physical appearance made him seem too young to fight in the one that mattered, and he had been powerless to do anything more than look on in horror and sadness at the tremendous loss resulting from the many that followed. So many. So senseless. What was today? Wednesday. *Wednesday's child is full of woe.* Another memory nagged at the corners of Pavel's mind and lingered there in some long-denied recess of his mind as he stood alone in his dark home.

He walked into the kitchen and to a door with stairs leading down to a root cellar. He turned on the light over the stairs and descended the few short steps to the cellar. The space was little more than a cleared area of the crawl space under the house, which Pavel had fashioned into a below-ground room common in the Midwest or parts of Europe, but unusual for sunny California. The smell of the rich dirt floor drifted into his nostrils, and he took a deep breath that seemed to start first at his toes, then travel up through his body and into his nostrils. He was somehow comforted by the odor of the rich, dry earth below his feet. He surveyed the various root vegetables stacked in fastidious and ordered fashion and selected a turnip for his Wednesday midday meal. Pavel always ate a turnip on Wednesday. Monday, he ate a parsnip. Tuesday, he would eat a rutabaga. *Monday's child is fair of face, Tuesday's child is full of grace.* The nagging memory persisted, but chose not to reveal itself in full; however, the fragment of the poem forced a slow melancholy into his emotions, though emotion for him had been drained and deadened over long years of solitude. A man in his position could not afford the circumstances that accompanied strong feelings of any kind, and years of grief and hurt had evolved in him a particular numbness that was neither a relief nor a comfort.

He came back up the steps into the kitchen, where he

took a magnet from the refrigerator and held it over the drawer front—a type of child lock he had installed years ago after one of the many earthquakes. No drawer could be opened without the magnetic key. He pulled the handle with a firm but frail hand, his hands now spotted and calloused by time and manual effort. He placed the magnet key back on the refrigerator and returned to the open drawer which held knives for every purpose. Slicing and filet knives, serrated and Santoku, meat and fish slicers, mincers and boning knives—all gleaming in their designated locations within the drawer. Pavel selected a simple paring knife. He made a long slice through the turnip with a deliberateness, his thumb providing the right amount of cushion at the end of the slicing action to collect the result. He took the first slice and put it in his mouth, tasting the bittersweet character of the root.

"Unloved vegetables," She had called them. He remembered something about Her laugh. She had been making fun of his sense of injustice which extended to include not only persecuted humans, but also certain vegetables shunned by the palate of the general public. His face crinkled into what might be considered a small smile at the memory, though his mind stumbled at remembering Her name or when She'd made the remark. He remembered only that She was important.

The old man carried the turnip and knife across the vintage tile floor of his immaculate kitchen, back into the living room, slicing off bits, putting them into his mouth and chewing as he walked. The smell and taste of the turnip livened his senses to other things in the old house. Sunlight hit his face as it snuck through in streaks where the windows had managed to escape cover by the special drapes, allowing undiffused light to enter the space. Odors entered his nostrils as he moved around the various pieces of furniture, long covered with white sheets to protect them from dust and time. Floor wax, lemon oil, white vinegar. Pavel kept a very neat home and while not averse to cleaning, he found covering things that remained unused to be easier on the amount of housekeeping required for such a large, old house. No housekeeper would enter the premises. They had made sure of that. Any cleaning must be done by Pavel alone. The mirrors that hung in the foyer and hallway had been draped in black cloth ever since…. The persistent nagging at his memory pushed him a little harder. Pavel tried to brush it away but the memory endured, and he was reminded of a time when the grocery delivery boy had come by. Pavel had opened the door that day in an act of… what, exactly? Rebellion? Madness? The boy glanced into the house from the open doorway and saw that the mirror mounted in the foyer, on the wall directly facing the front door, had been draped in black. He was not supposed to open the door to the boy, but he had not seen anyone in a very long time.

When had Pavel last opened that door… 1970, perhaps.

1970

"Are you Jewish?" the boy asked. Pavel stood to the side of the doorway, in the shadows created by his drapery.

"Jewish?"

"Did someone die?"

"Oh! Yes. Yes, I'm sorry. Yes, someone has died."

"I'm sorry for your loss."

"Thank you."

"My grandmother was Jewish," the boy said. "She told me you have to cover the mirrors."

"Ah, yes. What do I owe you today?" Pavel observed the boy, coltish in frame, his face in the beginning stages of an invasion by pimples. The boy's clothing—a striped shirt hanging over denim pants that flared wide at the feet and were much too long for his already long legs. Clothing styles for the youth had greatly altered since he had last seen a young person. His hair was full and long over the ears, and the lock that fell across the boy's forehead reminded Pavel of the forelock on a horse. In fact, there was much about the boy that reminded him of a horse, which caused him to feel a twinge of amusement.

"Nah, it's okay, sir. Mr. Hull wouldn't want me to charge you right now."

"Mister... Hull?"

"The grocer? Hey, listen, are you okay? Do you have anyone to sit Shiva with you?"

Pavel gaped at the boy who stood so concerned and earnest in his doorway.

"Shiva?"

"You know—"

"Oh! Yes, I'm sorry. Yes. I'm afraid I'm not thinking. I have apparently misled you. I'm not Jewish. My people are Czech—it's an old custom for us as well, I think. Actually, I think it might be a custom for a lot of people. Are you sure I can't pay you today?"

"Oh! I thought that—well, that's cool. But are you okay here? Do you have anyone staying with you?"

"My, but you are a curious and caring young man, aren't you? I'm fine, thank you. Thank you for coming by. You are very kind. Here is something for your trouble." Mr. Trusnik pressed a waxed paper envelope containing several bills into the boy's hand, far more money than would cover the cost of the groceries and a tip for the boy. Already wearing heavy, leather gloves, he took extra care to hold the waxed paper by a corner so as not to make contact with the boy's skin. The boy gazed in confusion at Pavel and his gloved hands.

"Please tell Mr. Hull I am most grateful to him." He shut the door in the boy's face and watched through the door's peephole until the boy walked down the front stairs of the porch, down the walk and out of his field of vision. He removed his gloves and placed them on the credenza nearest the door, then carried the box of groceries into the kitchen.

Pavel had spoken to an individual from the outside. The feeling of contact, albeit briefly, with another person left him overwhelmed, and he could feel his heart beat slightly faster than he was accustomed. No matter. He expected to receive a phone call soon about answering the door, since doing so was forbidden. Maybe they would ignore this transgression, since no one got hurt.

After that day, Pavel called a builder and paid for the construction of an anteroom that would allow delivery people access to an enclosed area which would serve as a barrier between the outdoors and indoors. When expecting a delivery, he would leave out money, along with instructions to make all deliveries without knocking. He was able, then, to collect his purchases without having to go out into the open.

He called it the "Mud Room."

"You'll be wanting a mud room, then?" asked the builder on the other end of the telephone.

Pavel held the phone to his ear and consulted a drawing he had made, currently spread on the kitchen table in front of him.

"A mud room?"

"Yeah. And you'll be wanting some shelves and hanger areas for the coats and boots and stuff, then?"

Pavel imagined shelves and hangers were designed for people coming in and going out of the main house. He would fill them with something for appearances.

"That sounds very nice. You send me the plans and I'll let you know."

"I can bring them by—"

"I prefer that you send them through the post."

Pavel did not intend to have any contact with the builder.

"You're the boss. The 'post' it is. And don't worry, Mr. Trusnik. We'll make it match the house. Beautiful old Victorian architecture, that. Italianate, isn't it?"

"You know your Victorians, sir."

"Sure do. Beautiful. Don't see too many of these places anymore. You see plenty of the Queen Annes and that sort of thing, but this…"

"I suppose that's true."

"And it's a darn shame. Who did your restoration—they did a beautiful job."

Pavel was becoming uncomfortable with the length of the conversation and with the questions.

"Oh, that was years ago, I have forgotten. It has been so nice talking to you. I look forward to seeing the plans."

Pavel hung up.

All deliveries were made to the Mud Room. People entered, left packages or other purchases, and Pavel collected them without ever venturing outside or coming into contact with anyone. Mr. Trusnik had been conducting business with the outside world that way for many years. Decades, perhaps. The length of time was impossible to remember or to comprehend.

Chapter 2

Present Day

A landscaping company came once a week to trim the yard. Sprinklers set with timers made hand watering the plants and flowers a thing of the past. Maintaining the garden had been easy when the house was new, but time and circumstance had complicated things. Pavel was grateful for the modern conveniences available to him, by either telephone or computer. He missed walking among the carefully selected plants in the front yard. Each had been picked to invite and celebrate as much life as the garden could accommodate—butterfly bushes, citrus, lavender, fuchsia, rue and rosemary, thyme and sage—all attracted a variety of bees, butterflies, birds, and a great many insects to Pavel's delight, season after season. A similar creation existed in the house's enclosed back yard. He'd not ventured outside for many years during the daylight hours to enjoy his creation, but he saved that pleasure for the hours when it was dark and the neighborhood asleep. Then, he could enjoy walking among the plants.

A house painting company had a standing appointment every five years to touch up the exterior of the Victorian so that Pavel's home would remain tidy and protected from the weather and would avoid any appearance of neglect. He opined that a poorly maintained home would draw far more attention than one that was treated with care. A well-established roofing company had a similar appointment to replace the roof every decade. One day, the Historical Preservation Society came by and embedded a plaque in the sidewalk in front of the house, designating the Victorian a historical landmark of the City of Pasadena.

"How nice," he thought, until he received a letter one day which stated that any alteration or addition that might compromise the historically protected landmark was forbidden under the guidelines set by the Historical Preservation Society. The letter also requested his consent to allow tours of the interior of the house as well as the back garden. He balked at that and sent a polite, but firm, refusal. The Society was quite persistent, and Pavel found it necessary to engage Mr. Trope. Mr. Trope was a weasel of a man with whom Pavel had been reluctantly obligated to form a business alliance many, many years prior. Mr. Trope, currently his attorney in addition to many other functions, was responsible for attending to the matter of his privacy and the rules of his isolation. Like the painters and roofers, Mr. Trope handled all of his affairs on retainer. He paid

Pavel's bills, made investments on his behalf and protected his overall interests. Mr. Trope was also responsible for ensuring that Mr. Trusnik adhered to the terms of his present arrangement regarding visitors or any ventures outside his home.

Pavel had carved out a regular routine that shunned all outside activity during the daylight hours. No one knocked on the door to ask to use the facilities or for a glass of water. If they did, Pavel stood on the other side of the door and stared through the peephole while the door remained unanswered. No neighbors came by to borrow the proverbial cup of sugar. Sales people and religious solicitors respected the sign out front that read "No solicitors please." Time and consistency on his part had made him, as well as the house, a cipher to be ignored. In the years preceding his present arrangement with Mr. Trope, Pavel made small trips out of doors to work in the front garden or to take short walks in his neighborhood. Certain visitors came, and he had lived a less solitary life. That changed the day the boys broke the window.

Wednesday's Child is full of woe. Pavel's memory had become like one of those round puzzle-ball toys used for teaching shapes to children—the kind that contained many different geometrically-shaped holes cut into the ball and into which identically shaped blocks could be inserted. Every now and then a shape would fall into place in his memory. At other times the empty places in his memory remained like the holes in the toy. The others had been worried about his memory. Should he be?

If his waning memory served, he was certain the baseball, propelled by the force of youthful strength and reckless exuberance, had crashed through the window on a Wednesday, shattering the leaded glass. He could not remember how many of the children he had come in contact with that day or how many arms he'd grabbed in his hurt and anger.

1942

"Throw it here, throw it here!" yelled the boy, his voice somewhat muffled by the leaded glass windows. Inside, Pavel could make out the voices at play outside in the street.

"Hey batter, batter, batter, what's the matter, batter, batter, batter…"

"Shut up!"

Crack.

"Oh no!" several voices cried at once.

The ball crashed through the glass of one of Pavel's front windows that faced the living room. The "parlor," She had called it. The window's shattering was followed by the breaking of glass in a framed daguerreotype photograph hung upon the wall, directly opposite the window. The photograph was the only one Pavel possessed of Her. The frame shattered and the daguerreotype along with it, as age had made the silvered, copper plate unstable and brittle.

"What have you done?" Pavel cried, running outside to confront the terrified boys in his front yard.

He thought about the one boy. The leader. Stuart had been his name. Why did he remember *that*?

The boys were all dead now, of course.

Chapter 3

Kevin: Present Day, Pasadena

Kevin sped along Marengo Avenue on his skateboard. The sight of a youth on a skateboard was commonplace in Pasadena, or about anywhere, for that matter. The skateboard provided the seventeen-year-old boy a useful means of getting around unobserved while he made it a point to observe *everything*. Especially the houses. Kevin adjusted the ear buds from his mp3 player and turned up the volume. What he heard made him smile.

"*No, please don't… I'm begging you. Why are you doing this?*"
"*Because I can.*"

Bloodcurdling screams filled his ears, and Kevin almost turned down the volume but decided to keep it loud. No one was around to hear what he listened to, and if anyone asked, Kevin had an easy explanation. The smell of copper and fear filled his memory, causing him to smile.

Kevin navigated the streets up to Fillmore, then Magnolia, and arrived at his house, a typically pricey Pasadena Craftsman on a street lined with other traditional Craftsman, Italianate, and Queen Anne Victorians for which Pasadena was known, along with the occasional condominium complex, more prevalent now, as the economy deteriorated. He kicked the skateboard into his arms, bounded up the front stairs and through the front door. He ran up the steps to his room where he deposited the skateboard, then moved down the hall to more stairs which led to the attic. Once in the attic, Kevin sat and stared out the window at the big Victorian across the street. Kevin made a point to stare at the Victorian across the street at a different hour every day, to see if the old man who lived there would come outside. Kevin had never seen anyone go in or come out of the house. He watched plenty of delivery trucks pull up in front and take packages or boxes into what appeared to be some sort of anteroom at the side of the house. Kevin figured that room led to another door that would connect to the interior. Kevin had never seen so much as a silhouette behind a moving drapery to indicate that a person might inhabit the house. The house might indeed be empty; however, everyone in the neighborhood seemed to know that an old man lived there. People claimed he had lived there as long as anyone could remember. Everyone said that, but no one could claim to have ever seen him. Kevin watched the myriad of delivery people, but did not see anyone who was not in some way connected with a company that was providing a service. They certainly did not appear to be friends or family. No one stayed longer than the time it would take to drop off the mail. The longest anyone stayed were the yard people who came to do the "mow, blow and go" type of gardening service common to the area. Their comings and goings, however did prove to Kevin that there was indeed someone inside to receive the numerous packages and boxes and food items, but in all his vigilance, Kevin never once saw the old man. Very little interested the teen, yet the curiosity Kevin felt toward the unseen resident across the street was overwhelming, similar to what an overzealous anthropologist might experience when discovering a completely new culture that had been hidden from modern society for years.

Kevin had watched the Victorian from the attic window every day for the past year, and he felt ready. The "music" on his mp3 player was beginning to bore him.

Kevin backed away from the attic window and moved to the floor and the roll of architectural blueprints. He'd acquired them at the local historical society after telling the nice lady at the counter he needed them for a school project on Pasadena Victorians.

"I absolutely *have* to have *that* Vic-*tor*-ian," he'd whined.

Kevin chuckled as he reflected on his power to annoy people into giving him what he wanted. Eventually, they all did. Their screams were a bonus.

Kevin was a Cage Rattler, one of those types of people at the zoo, or the aquarium or school who derive satisfaction from taunting the animals by pounding on the cage bars or the aquarium glass, or by tormenting fellow students too insecure or frightened to protect themselves. Some were plain lonely and thought they had made a new friend. The difference between Kevin and other Cage Rattlers was that Kevin had an insatiable curiosity to see how animals or people would behave under the most extreme of circumstances, usually violent, so tapping on the glass at the aquarium or pounding the cage bars was, to Kevin, a relatively benign experiment. He liked to take things apart to see how they worked, though taking apart games or electronics or machines held no interest for him. Kevin thought he would make a brilliant doctor. He liked his research. Sometimes the objects of his cruelty would inexplicably disappear, or in some instances, show up in an empty parking lot, dismembered. The animals' deaths were usually credited to either coyotes or practitioners of Santería, depending on when or where they were finally discovered. The shy students he chose from schools other than his own simply went "missing." Usually.

The first time Kevin ventured beyond the various neighborhood cats, dogs, and chinchillas even, often given to children as a fashionable alternative to rabbits——and once a tortoise that he later discovered was quite valuable—he focused his attention upon a child at one of the neighborhood grade schools; a small boy, playing off by himself. No friends, a little weird, a little off, thought Kevin.

"Hey kid. Do you like sour gummies?"

The child seemed to be so surprised that anyone noticed him, let alone spoke to him, that he was willing to go with Kevin, who handed the boy a sour gummy. The boy, eager for the candy, put it in his mouth and grinned. Kevin grinned back. The boy was small in build, with large brown eyes and close cropped hair—a buzz cut, some would call it. He was dressed in clothing inappropriate for any type of outdoor play. His clothes were so clean and neat; they appeared to have come straight from the dry cleaners, pressed and pristine.

"Do you like to climb trees? I know where there are a lot of good climbing trees. At the dog park."

"That park is closed. My mom said. Too much poop."

Kevin laughed. "That's right. Too much poop." The city had closed the dog park to do the annual seeding of the lawn, and the entire circumference of the grounds was enclosed in yellow warning tape. Kevin led the child as far as the entrance with the promise of the sour gummies.

"We're not supposed to be in here. I'll get dirty. Mom says I'm not supposed to get dirty."

"Well we can't very well get more sour gummies, then, can we? The tree elves hide them in the tops of the trees!"

The boy gawked at Kevin in wonder. Kevin grinned. "That's right. There are more sour gummies at the top of the tree."

Kevin put his hand around the boy's waist and hoisted him up to the crotch of the oak tree and jumped up after him.

"Don't worry, I've got you. We'll go to the top together."

"I'm not supposed to get dirty."

"You'll be fine. Have you ever seen a tree elf?"

The boy shook his head and continued to climb with Kevin, though he was unsteady, clumsy, almost falling at one point, but his new friend Kevin held onto him and helped him in his effort to make it all the way to the top of the tree.

Kevin's science class was covering Sir Isaac Newton that week and rather than read the assigned chapters on the discovery of gravity, he decided to take a more active approach to his homework. As he pushed the boy from the top of the tree, he recorded the sound the boy made while he was falling—the animalistic wail accompanied by the crashing of branches, the scrape of leaves and twigs tearing at the bare skin of the boy's face and arms—crows cawing in the air overhead and the grunt and exhalation of air as the boy landed on the ground and died from his injuries.

That was the first "music" Kevin recorded for his mp3 player.

The child was later discovered, scratched, broken and crumpled below the tree in the park. People went crazy in the belief that there was a child molester on the prowl, and every registered sex offender on the Megan's Law directory that lived within a fifty mile radius was brought in by the police for questioning. It was determined to be an accident, however. After an exhaustive investigation, the child was believed to have fallen from the tree after climbing up much too high and had died as a result of the fall. How or why the child had left school and gone to that park to climb the tree was a mystery that had not been solved.

Kevin had studied the blueprints over and over until he was sure he knew where each door, each window, each nook and cranny in all the rooms was located. The owner of the house had not filed permits with the city for any remodeling or additions, since the Victorian was under historical protection. Kevin noted that the anteroom on the side of the house where deliveries were made appeared to have been added forty years ago, but that was all. Kevin was confident he had what he needed.

Perhaps he would pay his neighbor a visit tonight. Tonight was as good as any. He had a few activities planned for earlier in the day, but the night held a host of great possibilities.

Kevin went down the stairs, out of the attic, then back into his room. Kevin's bedroom was a large room, with several expensive toys and games littering a built-in desk that ran along one wall, broke at the corner and extended at a right angle down the next wall. The room was immaculate because the housekeeper had cleaned it. Kevin surveyed the room and was grateful for the housekeeper's violation of his space, for it maintained the illusion that he had nothing to hide from his family. Kevin was aware that the housekeeper had been instructed to look for contraband of any kind. All the contraband was in the attic where he stored his true treasures. He'd stowed those treasures in a small duffle on the floor at his feet. Kevin kicked it under the bed, picked up his skateboard and bounded down the stairs and out the door. He had something he needed to do.

Chapter 4

Pavel watched out through the window as the boy across the street exited his home and rode away on his skateboard as he did every day. Pavel made an everyday habit of watching his neighborhood and the comings and goings of all the people in it. He watched through drapes that didn't move, because there was no need to open them when he could see out of them with such ease. He observed, year after year, the minutiae of the world outside. Sometimes he used a pair of opera glasses to increase his vision. He watched the little old ladies of Pasadena attempting to navigate cars too big for them to drive, making their way down the street in front of his house, or the children and teens coming and going into houses of the parent or parents that were responsible for them. One house at the end of the block had been converted into an inconspicuous halfway house for recovering drug addicts, the inhabitants thin, crushed, broken, hollow-eyed. Another house was inhabited by a young couple, and Pavel noticed the woman often wore turtleneck sweaters and sunglasses on sunny California days in an ineffective attempt to cover her bruises. He was not allowed to get involved, but thought he might write a letter to Mr. Trope about the woman in the turtleneck. He noticed other things as well, things that were supposed to go unnoticed. Secrets. So many people with things to hide, he thought, that could not stay hidden. Not to him. He watched everyone. He stood in his home, waiting for the day to end, for the dark to come and bring that hour when he could throw open the windows to let in the night air, that hour when he could step unseen into the walled garden at the back of the house. Then he could lift his face to the sky and feel the air, and breathe in the lingering odors of the day. This time of year, the strong aroma of phosphorous emanating from the plants and trees evoked memories of passion, of lovemaking, of Her. Sweat. Heat. The rise and fall of her petite body breathing in sleep afterward, while he watched her. Pavel stood among the shrouded furniture pieces and draped mirrors, lifted his chin and inhaled imagined night air. Another memory crept to the forefront of his thoughts: burying his face in the crook between Her neck and shoulder, biting in play as their bodies rose and fell together in complete and uninhibited passion.

Wednesday's child is full of woe, Thursday's child has far to go, Friday's child is loving and giving. He felt a sensation upon his face and reached up, ran his hand across the creases and furrows that made up the whole of his face. It had been smooth once. He touched something wet. Was it a tear? He could not be sure. He remembered having cried numerous times over the course of his life, but he could not recall when, if ever, he had experienced anything approaching tears in the last years. Why today would be different than any other was a bit of a curiosity to him. Another tear escaped from his eye to run unbidden down his face, leaving a drop upon his fastidiously laundered cardigan. A feeling of great remorse threatened to move closer to the front of his memory, which he took haste to dismiss.

Pavel was sure of one thing. He had lived for almost three hundred years, but had loved fully and deeply only once. And now he was having difficulty remembering Her name.

Chapter 5

1714

Pavel was a mere three years old when the people in his family and their village fell ill with the plague. A major outbreak occurred and would claim the lives of over ten thousand people. The plague was the last horrific disease to which people succumbed after being stricken by a series of other mysterious illnesses and deaths in the days following Pavel's arrival in the world. The thriving collection of villages near Pavel's, filled with families, children, farms, and merchants, all sickened over time. First cholera, then the wasting sickness—sometimes referred to as consumption, then more dysentery. Following those more minor, yet devastating illnesses, the plague let loose on the entire area, leaving waste, stink, blood, pain, coughing spasms, oozing wounds and finally death. Pavel's first years were filled with one gruesome loss after another, the first being his mother who died during childbirth. The aunt who had served as his wet nurse following the death of his mother died soon after. His sisters died closely after that. The more superstitious among the villagers likened the series of illnesses to "vampirism," and when the first deaths occurred, the corpses were burned. The villagers buried the bones with the skull placed between crossed leg bones so that the dead could not reassemble and chew their way out of their graves.

The priest who baptized Pavel was the next person to die. The remaining villagers who were not yet ill began to look at the toddler with suspicion, though he was a defenseless and affectionate young boy who hugged and kissed anyone who came in contact with him. Their distrust was replaced with complete hysteria on the day that Pavel's father, a stern and unaffectionate man, died, the last of the family, leaving the small boy an orphan.

"The child is cursed!" claimed many.

"A changeling!" cried others.

"A vampire child!"

Rather than put the child in a bag and drown him in the river, as had been demanded by many, the village clergy and doctors gave Pavel a series of examinations. Amidst clouds of incense and burning herbs, Pavel's small body and head were poked, prodded and talked over. One of the first discoveries given significance by the examiners was the existence of two unexplained scars, one over each shoulder blade. Someone had removed two growths of some sort during Pavel's infancy, and the areas had been stitched up with an inexpert hand. The clergy and doctor found no one still alive who might be able to explain the scars.

"Could his father have done this?"

"The midwife?"

"They might be the horns of a demon!" cried one terrified examiner.

"May I remind you this is an innocent child who has been baptized," cautioned a clergyman.

"That don't make 'im an angel," said another.

Having no family to protect or stand up for him, the affectionate child became the beaten child. Many villagers took out their anger, fear and frustration upon the boy with sticks, rocks, broomsticks or the occasionally thrown shoe. He remained a source of fear and curiosity, while those around him continued to sicken and die. Pavel no longer hugged or kissed people, but rather cowered when they came near and did his best to avoid contact with anyone.

Arguments over Pavel and what to do with him came to an end when no one was left in the village. A passing traveler discovered Pavel wandering alone on the dusty trail, miles from where he lived. No one was left where Pavel came from, so no one knew who he was or where he called home. He was deposited by the traveler, who did not need an additional mouth to feed, at the infirmary of the nearest orphanage, where he was fed and given clothing, but never held or touched or loved. Pavel had become so fearful of the beatings that he was fine with the lack of contact. People feared the lone child found wandering the countryside with the strange scars on his back. Pavel remained at the orphanage until he was five when he was deemed old enough to live with and work for one of the local merchants. Pavel's first job was sweeping out a bakery. Though still a small boy, Pavel knew that he was fortunate to be at the bakery instead of one of the factories, or going in and out of the chimneys, like some of the other small boys. The boys from the factories and chimneys resembled ghosts. To Pavel, they were no longer boys, but the shadows of boys. He did not want to end up a shadow. In a few short years following Pavel's apprenticeship to the baker, he was removed and sent to what he thought was to be a lumber factory near the center of the city of Prague. He was afraid of the factory, and thought that his days as a ghost were soon before him.

"They call me Prochazka" said the large, red-faced man, who seemed to be inspecting the little boy.

"I am Pavel," said the boy.

"Pavel. Well, Pavel, you are a young man of few words. That will serve us well in the workshop. I'll need you to shut up and to listen to me. Can you do that?"

Pavel looked through wide eyes at the large man and remained silent.

"Have you ever chopped wood?"

Pavel, afraid to speak, shook his head.

"Well, we will have to teach you to do that, yes?"

Pavel thought about the boys and girls that went into the factories or those he saw climbing in and out of the chimneys and imagined himself becoming one of them: skin gray, eyes lifeless, hungry. He raised his head high to show the large man he was not afraid.

"Very good. Have you ever seen puppet theatre?"

Pavel nodded.

"And where was that?"

Pavel had no idea why this man was asking him about puppets. What did that have to do with chopping wood?

"It's all right. Speak, child," said Prochazka.

"I worked in the square. I was sweeping out the bakery across from the plaza where they had the show."

"Do you remember what it was?"

"No. I didn't understand it."

The large man cocked his head and leveled a hard gaze at Pavel.

"Did you like it, even if you did not understand it?"

Pavel was not sure how to respond.

"It is not a trick question. Was the show enjoyable? Did you smile?" Prochazka asked.

"I liked it," responded Pavel.

"Good. You'll be creating them in no time!"

"What?" Pavel did not understand.

"Well someone has to *make* them. They aren't born—not like you were, anyway."

"My mother died when I was born, they tell me," said Pavel.

The man calling himself Prochazka softened his voice and stooped down so that he could face Pavel rather than look down upon him.

"Well, they tell me that happens to a lot of people, Pavel. I expect you are in good company. Would you like to make puppets with me?"

"You make puppets?" Pavel asked.

"And so shall you," said Prochazka.

Pavel was thoroughly confused.

"I thought I was to work for a man at a lumber factory."

"Well, we use lumber, yes. But I hope it is a little more than that. We *manipulate* lumber." Prochazka laughed out loud. Pavel did not understand the large man or why he laughed. Pavel went back to staying silent, watching.

Thus began Pavel's apprenticeship at the age of seven to Prochazka—maker of traditional puppets for the Czech theatre.

"You can put your things here, though it doesn't look like you have much," Prochazka said to Pavel and pointed at a small room with a bed and a chest of drawers. "There's a pot under the bed for you to relieve yourself. You're responsible for cleaning that out. I'll show you where to take it." They had reached the room by walking through an enormous cavern of work tables and lumber and tools. The space seemed vast to Pavel. It smelled of sawdust, glue and resin. Hundreds of puppets hung from the ceiling and from hooks on the walls. Others were draped over workbenches and chairs. Miles of fabric, tulle, and lace were piled on one table, and women sat in a corner and sewed, while men with chisels and saws stood at the tables working on pieces of wood. The women contemplated Prochazka and the boy when they entered and watched without smiling as he led the boy to his new room. Prochazka picked up a marionette from a workbench and walked it behind Pavel, copying Pavel's walk.

"This is Sammy, the Redheaded Weird Boy," said Prochazka. "He's a very bad actor, so I can't put him in any of the shows, but if I give him to you, maybe you'll be able to teach him a thing or two. Would you like to do that?"

Pavel was mesmerized by the puppet. "Sammy, the Redheaded Weird Boy—what kind of name is that?" Pavel asked.

"The right one. Look at him!" said Prochazka.

"Hmm." Pavel could see he had a point. The marionette was an odd looking distribution of arms and legs, and its crooked painted face was topped by a fright of long red hair woven from thick yarn.

Prochazka manipulated the puppet to walk behind Pavel as they entered the room. Pavel put his small roll on the bed and turned to face Prochazka. Prochazka removed one hand from the control of the marionette and extended it as if to place his hand on the boy's shoulder. Pavel stepped back.

"What's wrong, Pavel?" asked Prochazka.

"You better not touch me. They told you about me? I'm some sort of monster, they tell me."

"Who says this about you?" said Prochazka, alarmed.

"The orphanage. Everyone. The bakery owner where I was before here. They call me a demon and say I make people sick. They say I killed my family." The young Pavel stated all of this with a matter-of-fact intensity that was far beyond his few years.

Prochazka studied the boy for what seemed a very long time, and once again reached out to the boy in an attempt to reassure him. Pavel winced and moved away.

"The plague killed your family, boy. See? I'm fine," said Prochazka.

"But—"

"I'll tell you what I heard. I heard that you might be one of my puppets, escaped and let loose in the world, that's what I heard."

"What?" Pavel stared wide-eyed at the large man.

"That's right. They said, 'We have this boy. He sits there until you tell him what to do, and he does it. Just like you tell him. And he never smiles. He's some sort of puppet. He even has scars on his back from where the strings used to be. We think he escaped from your shop, that's what we think,'" said Prochazka.

"Who... who told you that?" asked Pavel.

"Oh, everyone and anyone. Or no one. You can never be sure when people are talking about escaped puppets. They all lie. Are you an escaped puppet? What do you think, Sammy, is the boy an escaped puppet?"

"Could be," said Sammy, as intoned by Prochazka.

Pavel laughed for the first time. "No, that's silly!"

"Ah! So you *can* laugh. You see? They all lie. May I see the scars? Would that be all right?"

Pavel was frightened, but he had learned that it was best to do as he was told. He had learned that at the end of many a broomstick when he was still at the orphanage, and again, at the bakery. Pavel did not mind being touched, nor did he believe that he could make people sick by touching them. That did not make sense. He did not like to be touched when the touch became a beating. He turned his back on Prochazka and removed his tunic. Prochazka said nothing. Pavel turned and faced the large man who looked very sad.

"Well, it seems that someone might be telling the truth. You may indeed be an escaped puppet. Someone cut your strings, it does appear. I wonder who would do that sort of thing. What do you think about that, Pavel?"

"You're not telling the truth."

"Maybe, maybe. But now that you're here, who better to apprentice in a puppet workshop than an escaped puppet, I ask you? I think that's marvelous! Isn't that marvelous, Sammy?" Sammy shook his head in wild abandon, his red yarn hair flying in every direction. Prochazka let out a big laugh and moved to pat Pavel on the shoulder, yet again. Pavel moved away and put his tunic back on.

Prochazka manipulated Sammy closer to Pavel. "I think Sammy would like to pat you on the shoulder—I think that would be okay." Sammy did a little dance and waved his arms in a jerky fashion, and the expression painted upon his face gave him the appearance of insanity.

"No," said Pavel, though he did find the puppet to be very funny.

"Very well, Puppet Pavel. You do not wish to be touched. And so you won't be. We are artists here, and artists respect each other, even if no one else will!" He laughed again. "We eat in an hour. There is a lavatory for washing up on the other side of the workshop. I suggest you get yourself cleaned up. You look like you haven't seen a cake of soap in quite a while—can't have you coming to the table a dirty puppet, now can we?"

"I'm not a puppet!" exclaimed Pavel.

"We shall see, we shall see," said Prochazka. The large man glanced toward the boy, then shook his head and placed Sammy the Redheaded Weird Boy down on the bed, He returned to the workshop where he sat at a workbench with his back to the boy, bent over a piece of wood and began to chisel.

Pavel examined the puppet on his bed. He believed

this was the first time he had received a gift of any kind, and he made a promise in his head to Prochazka that he would take great care of it. He wondered how Prochazka had made it walk like that, like him.

Pavel went across the workshop to the lavatory—a small and narrow room where a pitcher of water was placed next to a large bowl on top of a long table. Someone had filled the pitcher with water and he poured from it into the bowl beside it. A mirror hung on the wall over the table. A large basin sat on the ground, and Pavel guessed it was used for bathing. The orphanage infirmary had a similar one, and he'd been allowed to use it, once. This particular one was stained from the dyes used for the costumes. He peered around the lavatory for a cloth to wipe his face and noticed a shelf under the long table that contained cloths for washing and drying. He picked one. A cake of soap was already in the bottom of the bowl, ready to be used. Pavel got to work and cleaned the grime from his head, face, neck and shoulders. The water felt warm on Pavel's face. He removed his tunic and washed his torso. He faced his reflection in the mirror and ran his fingers through his hair until it looked more presentable. He wished he had a comb. Curious, Pavel turned his back to the mirror and twisted his neck around as far as it would reach so that he could see the scars. There were two of them—one over each shoulder blade. He couldn't reach them with his hands to scratch the scars where they'd gotten bumpy and hard and often itched. He saw where the stitches had pierced his skin, white lines that crossed over one another. He did not know why they were there. The nurses in the infirmary had whispered about them but he was never able to understand their words. During his sweeping job at the plaza bakery, the owner had needed Pavel and had come into the small alcove where he slept. Pavel had his shirt off. The owner chased him from the bakery with a broom, and Pavel grabbed his few belongings as he ran, but not before the baker landed a few good whacks across Pavel's backside.

"Leave here, devil! Don't come back!"

Was Prochazka right that he was an escaped puppet? Maybe he did not remember. No, that was silly. You would remember something like that. Pavel put on his tunic and went into the workshop. A plump, pretty woman stood with Prochazka, her brown hair pinned in a messy fashion so that strands hung around her face and down her back. She regarded him with eyes that were such a pale blue, they were almost clear, like lights. A huge smile spread across her face.

"Sasha, you didn't tell me he was such a small boy!" The woman approached Pavel with her arms outstretched.

"Come here, you dear thing!"

Pavel stood frozen, terrified.

"Nina, leave the boy alone. Not yet. You'll frighten him."

"Oh, how ridiculous."

"Nina. Stop. Give the boy some time."

Prochazka spoke to the boy. "Pavel, this is my wife, Nina. She is quite excited to meet you, as you can see. We do not have a lot of children around here other than the puppets and she has never met an actual *escaped* puppet before. Isn't that right, Nina?"

"Oh, would you stop," said Nina.

"Pavel, I wonder if you would do Nina the kindness of showing her where they cut off your strings?"

"I'm not a puppet." Pavel said, frightened, remembering the bakery owner and the broom. "I haven't done anything wrong."

"Of course not! My wife has a tendency to not believe anything I say, and she is perhaps correct in that, because as I told you, everyone lies when it comes to talking about escaped puppets, so I wanted to show her proof that not only can puppets escape, but they can become handsome young boys."

Pavel awaited a sign from Prochazka, who motioned for Pavel to lift his garment. Pavel did what he was told, though it frightened him to have his back to them. He turned around and pulled his garment up over his shoulders, enough to show her the scars. He heard a sharp intake of breath behind him, and he flinched, waiting for the familiar crack of the broom across his back. Nothing happened.

"That's alright, Pavel, you may put your clothing back on. I'm starved! What do you think, Nina, should we have something to eat? Shall we feed this young puppet who has found his way home?"

Nina's gaze traveled from her husband to Pavel and back again. Pavel thought she might be crying, but she ran her hand across her eyes and smiled at him.

"Of course! He looks like he could use some fattening up. What do you think, Pavel? Are you hungry?" She stepped toward him then stopped herself.

"Pavel has said he does not like to be touched, Nina. I think we can respect that, yes? He has to come to trust us," said Prochazka.

"Yes. Yes, of course. Follow me when you are ready to eat."

Nina walked out, but first put her hand on her husband's arm, searched his eyes with her own, then patted Prochazka's large face before walking out the door that led to their living space.

"You'll be safe here, Pavel," said Prochazka, his eyes following his wife as she exited. "You do not have anything to worry about."

"I'm not a puppet," said Pavel.

"I know, my dear boy. I know. But allow us our little story, eh? It's a good one." Prochazka walked to the door, motioning for the boy to follow him.

Chapter 6

Present Day

Pavel sighed and ambled into the spacious kitchen, pristine in its historic authenticity and unsullied by modern makeovers and granite countertops. He put a kettle on the antique iron range in preparation of a cup of tea. He then turned on a small stereo unit on the counter, the one piece of modernity in the room. Mozart's *Nocturne No. 4 in A Major* wafted from unseen speakers recessed into the ceiling overhead, the various speakers installed by his expert hand. He had made some alterations over time to the house without a moment's thought to the people at the Historical Preservation Society. He loved this particular Mozart *Nocturne* which managed to be hopeful, yet melancholy at the same time. He stood at the sink and through the kitchen window he surveyed the house across the street, while he finished the last of his turnip. He cleaned the paring knife until it gleamed again, unlocked and returned it to the drawer as he studied the house opposite his own. He examined the other knives in the drawer and sighed. He turned off the music. Tonight's venture into the back garden and all of its accompanying comfort, aromas and memories would have to wait, for there was to be an unwelcome visitor. He had to prepare.

Dear Mr. Trusnik:

It has been brought to our attention that recent inquiries into the architectural blueprints of your home have been made and that said blueprints have been reproduced and removed from the Office of Historical Records. We regret the intrusion into your privacy. Our firm takes pride in making every effort to prevent these types of indiscretions. Please be advised that we are taking measures to acquire the copies, and that the lapse in judgment on the part of the staff at the Office of Historical Records has been dealt with. We will keep you apprised of any further information on this matter.

Sincerely,
Leonard Trope, III
Senior Partner
Trope & Co., LLP

"People are foolish," Pavel mused as he walked to the back of his house and through the doorway of his workroom.

The workroom was a high-ceilinged, vast space located at the very rear of the large house. A work table stretched the entire expanse of one wall, and connected with another table that went through the center of the room at a right angle. Every conceivable tool needed by a woodworking enthusiast, from antique to modern, hung from a pegboard mounted on the wall over the work table: band saws, drills, planes, numerous chisels—short ones, flat ones, stronger ones, fine ones—hammers, pliers, pots of glue and colored paint and brushes in myriad sizes and shapes. Situated around the room were easels of different sizes displaying unfinished canvases. Also present were tools and equipment designed for shoe repair and leatherwork as well as a pottery wheel and kiln. Shelves holding various bits of pottery and clay figurines lined any wall space not taken up by the tool pegboard. The principal occupants of the room, however, hung from ceiling hooks or lay upon the shelves in various states of repose. Some sat in chairs, as if to relax and have a conversation. Dozens upon dozens of hand-made marionettes and puppets of all designs and sizes filled the room. Some were controlled by wires, others by rods, and some by both. Dancers, jesters, peasant figures, cats and dogs— some were lifelike in appearance, while others were skeletons, or figures of a macabre nature. Puppets in various stages of finish covered the work tables.

"Hello, my dears," he said aloud to the room.

On the opposite side of the workroom, natural light spilled in from floor-to-ceiling windows that overlooked the back garden. In this room, Pavel could enjoy the sight of his garden through the great windows as he worked on his various creations during the daylight hours. Heavy curtains remained drawn on the days that the gardeners were scheduled and on any other occasion that required an outsider's presence. Years had gone into the creation of the large space where Pavel spent the majority of his days. It was in this place where he allowed himself to experience a modicum of joy.

He surveyed the windows. If he concentrated his gaze across the garden while standing at a forty-degree angle to the gardening shed, a bounce of reflected light and an accident of architecture enabled him to see into the kitchen of his home through one of the windows. Because the workshop at the back of the house was located at a ninety-degree angle to the back of the kitchen, he had discovered the ability to look from the workroom into his kitchen whenever the lights were extinguished. The ability to see into the kitchen had been useful on at least one occasion when the soup on the stove had bubbled over the pot. The light from the back window of the kitchen bounced a reflection off the window of the workshop, and if he faced the gardening shed and used it as a backdrop, he could see into the other part of the house. Odd, but it decreased the need for a surveillance system. Of course the lighting had to be correct for the effect to work, and he planned on turning off the main power to the house this evening. He sighed again.

Pavel turned on another small stereo located on the workbench. Chopin's *Mazurkas for Piano* floated from more unseen speakers which produced an auditory illusion that the room was filled with music from everywhere and nowhere, all at once. He felt a sudden chill and pulled his cardigan around his slight and stooped frame, buttoned the top three buttons and turned off the music. He did not want to hear

Chopin today and had only turned on the music to ensure the speakers were operational. He would have need for them later. Pavel had, over time, built a network of speakers all over the house. Due to the historic nature of the house, the walls and ceiling had to maintain the appearance of the original architecture, so he had made the speakers invisible by using scrims, various forms of muslin, and other painted fabrics to create sections of wall and ceiling indistinguishable from the rest of the house. The scrims hid metal grids which supported a large number of mounted speakers, each approximately six feet from the next. He designed the system to create an experience of sound without any discernible point of origin. The auditory effect was that music, or sound of any variety of his choosing, would seem to come from one or multiple directions. The idea was a deliberate construction meant to produce something alternately soothing or disorienting. If voices alone were played, the aural effect was that of disembodiment—almost like a haunted house. He had spent over a year on the concept alone and took great pains over the details of his construction, which took another year to complete. With the digital controls, he could manipulate the speakers by turning some off and others on, much like working with a puppet. Both actions involved a certain amount of artistry and a lot of expert skill. He designed it for his own entertainment, but his design had the ulterior purpose of being a very unconventional security system.

Pavel moved to a location at the end of the extensive work bench. A pedestal with the marionette of a boy, about four feet tall, faced the bench.

"Hello, David," he said. He was met with the silent

stare of the boy marionette.

"Ladies, how are we today?" He addressed three crone marionettes who looked as if they might have been used in a theatrical production of *Macbeth*. More silence.

The workbench was covered with a collection of wire mesh, metal pieces and other bric-à-brac in a large and messy jumble, inconsistent with the meticulous care reflected in the appearance of the rest of the room. Pavel reached into the mess and picked out an object. An animal snare. In the metal of the snare, he caught a slivered reflection of his cracked, spotted face and the thin hair that hung in limp, yellowed and worm-like tendrils across his head. He once had been agreeable to look upon. He put the snare under his arm and pulled out a large net from the mess of wires.

"That should be sufficient. What do you think, David?" Again, he received no answer.

"No?" He searched the table until his eyes lit upon the last thing he would need. A coil of razor wire. *Why did I buy this?* he wondered. No matter. He added the razor wire to his collection of items and spoke to the marionette he called David.

"What do you think of my dangerous collection?" He was met with more silence from the various marionettes that filled the space. He stood in the vast workroom, his arms full of his strange collection of objects, as the poem crept back into his mind.

Wednesday's child is full of woe, Thursday's child has far to go. He brushed the poem from his thoughts, for he had work to do, yet the poem persisted.

Thursday's child has far to... He seemed incapable of denying the poem access to his head and buzzing around his memory like an annoying and aggressive wasp. He could not place the importance of the poem, but the bits and pieces that insisted upon inserting themselves caused a sting.

Pavel was not without resources. His memory was not what it was in certain areas, and while certain sections of his past seemed to be hiding behind other sections more accessible to his aging mind, his brain did still work and his body had not failed him. His muscle memory seemed to make up for what he could not remember. Decade after decade of discipline and routine was so ingrained in him that there was little chance, even if he lost his mind, that he would vary from his way of doing things. He had full capability to draw upon any of his extensive skills at any time. He knew he was more than able to look up the source of the poem that stung every time a line invaded his thoughts; however, he did not want to. He had numerous books and references to consult the origin of the poem, had he been so inclined. In fact, any shelf not inhabited by a tool or a puppet held a book of some kind. Something nagged at him, however, and the thought of investigating the source of his torment worried him.

Modern technology had made Pavel's solitary state rather easy. He had a computer and access to the Internet. He ordered most of his deliveries over the Internet because anything he needed for the workshop could be ordered online, even items only available from overseas. Had it not been for the computer, he would never have been able to obtain the materials necessary to install his impressive network of digitally controlled speakers, nor the components necessary for the manufacture of the accompanying control board. The first time he ordered anything over the computer, he marveled at the advanced level which humans had reached in their ability to avoid interaction with other people. Through the use of technology, everyone could live, if they so desired, like Pavel—cut off from connection, communication and touch. He had increasing difficulty remembering why he lived like that but knew that he had for a very long time. The poem might shed some light on why he thought he should live in isolation, but remembering those nagging bits and pieces might cause him further distress. He had other things to concentrate on at present. An uninvited guest would be arriving soon.

"People are foolish," he repeated to himself. There had been other uninvited guests in the early years. The years before Her. Prochazka and Nina had protected him, and when Prochazka became old, he'd made a great effort to teach Pavel how to protect himself from people who were foolish.

Chapter 7

1735

"Bring out the demon!" An angry mob gathered outside the home of Prochazka and Nina. Many carried torches, others carried sticks, clubs or farming tools. Another cholera epidemic had laid waste to much of the community. Lack of proper sewage and the dumping of waste into the river Vltava made the drinking water a source of outbreaks. The terrified people sought blame on supernatural forces, and often that blame fell on those in the community who were *different*. Other. People who were not getting sick. Prochazka and Nina got all their drinking and cooking water from their own well. They emptied the chamber pots several meters away from the residence in a large hole that Prochazka had built in the ground with a structure around it that kept any person from falling in it. Prochazka would, at varying times throughout the year, cover up the hole and dig another elsewhere. Being a practical and smart man, he poured lye into the hole, thus reducing the odor and the possibility of filth spreading elsewhere. Prochazka and Nina kept a clean home and an even neater workshop at the theatre. The couple had a rational approach to maintaining order. While the rest of the town fell ill and many died, they remained healthy. This caused others to be suspicious, rather than curious about Prochazka, Nina and the strange adopted child in their home, Pavel. Many in the village thought them unnatural creatures who cheated illness and death—Pavel was a thirty-one-year-old man who appeared to be a youth of about thirteen years. Prochazka and Nina explained, on numerous occasions to villagers who never tired of asking, that the boy was stunted and did not grow at a normal rate. That explanation was irrelevant to the terrified townspeople who fell ill, or who were still well enough but had become desperate and irrational.

"You people are insane and you are imbeciles!" Prochazka came out of his home, bellowing. The mob moved toward him, ready to storm the house, but unsure of themselves once confronted by the large, red-faced man. "That boy has done nothing to you! If you people would stop drinking your own shit, maybe you would stop getting sick. Did that occur to anyone?"

"The boy is a hobgoblin!" said one.

"He carries the marks of the Devil on him!" said yet another.

"He protects you because you have made promises to

the Devil!" The mob grew nearer to the door.

"No one is to harm one hair on that boy's head. No one is harming anyone today! You are all fools!" Prochazka ran back into the home and hoisted the large pot from the stove filled with boiling water. He hefted it to the doorway.

"*This* is why we are not sick!" Prochazka heaved the scalding water out the door, splashing some of the mob as he did so. There were a few screams.

"We boil our fucking water, you idiots!" The people moved away from the large, red-faced man and then away from the house.

That particular evening Nina, Prochazka and Pavel remained safe.

Chapter 8

Kevin: Present Day

Kevin thought about his last house. A modest two-story tract home located among an inordinate number of other modest two-story tract homes in a housing development off the Antelope Highway. Kevin did not live there, and his family did not own the house; however, his memory of it and what happened there gave him a certain feeling of ownership. The "music" from that house had a special place in the playlist on his mp3 player.

Kevin happened upon the house quite by accident. In an ongoing bit of theatrics on his part, he participated in school events and activities like any other high school senior. That day, Kevin had travelled to the area along with a bus full of his fellow students to cheer for the football team at an away game. Kevin sat in the bus at a window seat but did not pay attention to the hills covered with row after row of housing subdivisions. Each development blended into the next with hundreds of identical houses on identical streets with identical mailboxes and lawns and front doors and homeowner associations with requirements that each and every dwelling remain indistinguishable from the hundreds surrounding it. Kevin's attention was suddenly stimulated, and he sat up, paying closer attention to what lay beyond the window. Kevin smiled. A plan began to form in his mind, a spontaneous bit of fun to break up the boredom of yet another football game.

Kevin had not brought his usual set of tools, but he was not concerned, as improvisation was second nature to him. The set of tools was at home in its special place in the attic, but he had ones he could work with. He had his skateboard, a watch to let him know what time to be back at the bus, a small, digital tape recorder of the kind used for dictation, and the most important tool of all, his scalpel which he kept on his person at all times. He had stolen it from the station next to his in the science lab when they were dissecting fetal pigs for Physiology class. He kept the scalpel in his pocket, wrapped in a square of leather cut for the purpose of keeping the scalpel safe and covered to prevent accidental injury or worse, loss of the scalpel through a hole in his pocket. His school was one of the few in the greater Los Angeles area that had not installed metal detectors, and students also were allowed the luxury of a locker. A student could carry or hide about anything. Sure, occasional locker inspections occurred, but Kevin never kept anything in his, other than what he needed for his classes. In fact, had faculty paid attention during the random inspections, the *lack* of items in Kevin's locker might have set off an alarm. His locker contained no pictures, notes, messages from friends, party invitations, clothing items—nothing personal to tie the individual to the locker other than the required textbooks and school supplies.

Kevin exited the bus with his fellow students. He blended into the crowd that rushed to the football field and the bleachers. He ducked under the bleachers, came out the other side and walked back out through the fence near the porta-potties brought in for the game. Kevin hopped on his skateboard and sped away from the crowd. No one paid attention to one boy on a skateboard moving away from the crowd. Kevin noted that the parents and students from the other school seemed to reflect the same nature as their houses—no one stood out from anyone else. No one expected anyone to stand out from anyone else. Kevin depended upon this to camouflage himself.

Kevin rode up and down identical streets through the suburban development, looking in front windows for signs of people at home. Many people were home for dinner, and Kevin watched them through dining room or kitchen windows. None of the occupants glanced out the window at him. No one appeared to notice the teenager on a skateboard at dusk. Other houses appeared to be unoccupied, the families out perhaps for a Friday night pizza or at the local game.

Kevin pointed at inhabited houses that were flanked by houses where no one appeared to be home. "Eenie, meenie, mynie, mo…." He rode his skateboard over the curb, onto the sidewalk, up the front walk of the house, and jumped off the skateboard as he arrived at the front door. He placed the skateboard behind a hibiscus bush planted near the front door and knocked.

A woman answered the door.

"Hi, are you Mrs. Williamson? I'm Kevin. Are my parents here?"

Kevin saw no reason not to use his real name.

"No, I'm afraid you have the wrong house."

Kevin noticed that the woman answering the door had the same appearance as many of the other women he had seen at the football game. Bobbed haircut, pastel sweater set, khaki pants. He wondered if the homeowners' association required that people look as identical to each other as their houses.

"Oh no! You wouldn't believe this, but this is the fifth house I've been to. I'm sooooo lost. My mom is so gonna kill me."

"I don't know anyone named Williamson, I'm sorry." The woman started to shut the door.

"My parents are here somewhere."

"No—"

She was getting impatient with him. Kevin could hear noises from the rest of the house.

"Oh, I don't mean your house. I mean they are at dinner at some friend of my mom's and I was supposed to meet them to eat before the game."

"The game at the high school?"

"Yeah. I am in so much trouble."

"Don't you have a cell phone?"

Kevin gave her a big, embarrassed smile. "No, would you believe it? My parents don't think kids should have those.

My mom says she's afraid I'll use it for sexting."

The woman appeared uncomfortable.

"I know, right? Gross, much?" Kevin had her. She would be thinking about that and nothing else, and it would never occur to her to ask anything logical, like did he know the name of the street where his parents were having dinner.

"Do you think I could use your phone?"

A man came to the door to stand behind the woman. "Who's this?"

The man was tall, wearing a polo shirt and khaki pants, like his wife. Unbelievable, Kevin thought.

"I'm Kevin. I was asking your wife if I could use your phone. I'm lost. I'm trying to find my parents who are at the Williamson's. All the houses here look the same—whose idea was that?"

The man laughed. "We get that a lot. Sure. Come on in."

Kevin walked into the entry and first heard, then saw two small children in the living room, playing a game on the television. They did not look up when he came in, engrossed in their game. Kevin smiled and put his hand in his pocket where the scalpel was tucked away in its neat square of leather.

There would be good music here tonight.

Kevin skateboarded back to the school, his hair still wet from his shower. He ducked in at the fence next to the porta-potties, then back under the bleachers and out the other side, just as everyone jumped to their feet in a cheer. He checked the scoreboard to see who was doing what, then moved up the bleachers to blend in with everyone for the final minutes of the game. He felt something on his cheek and wiped it off. Blood? Perhaps some dripped on him from the ceiling as he exited the front door.

On the bus ride home, Kevin smiled. The team had won and anyone might assume Kevin was proud of the team's success. Kevin knew that no one suspected that, tucked in the midst of hundreds of identical houses, was a house with a family that had come to a very violent and frightening end. The late news might cover the story, Kevin thought, or the morning news, whenever someone got around to finding them. Another horrible murder-suicide, they would report. Kevin thought about the "music" he would be adding to his mp3 player when he got home.

"No, please don't… I'm begging you. Why are you doing this?"
"Because I can."

Then the screaming. Such beautiful, beautiful screaming.

Chapter 9

1750

"I am an old man, and there are things we need to discuss." Prochazka had come to Pavel's room one morning and sat on the chair near the bed, looking very serious.

"You are not old," responded Pavel.

Pavel was a boy of about seven when he came to Prochazka and Nina. That was thirty-three years ago, though Pavel appeared to be no older than a boy in the beginning of his teenage years. Prochazka and Nina had told him he was "stunted," that he would not grow at the same rate as other people. Prochazka, however, was in his seventies, a very old man for the time. Pavel grew at a snail's pace, while Prochazka and Nina turned gray, then wrinkled, then thinned in build and stooped at the shoulder, palsied at the hand. Pavel had to do many things for them that they were unable to do for themselves anymore. He did not mind. He loved Prochazka and Nina. They were his world.

Prochazka wiped his hand over his eyes.

"Is everything all right, Táta?" Pavel used the familiar term for "Father" with Prochazka, as he had for many years.

"You know we are not religious people."

"What is wrong?"

"Hear me out, son."

Pavel sat and waited for his father to speak.

"We are people of the theatre. We make magic. We make things that cannot be explained by other people, to dazzle and entertain. Our lives are filled with the knowledge and ability to make bits of cloth and wood and paint appear to be flying unicorns or devils from underground or rainy skies on a sunny day. We do this for our audience. We know, however, that it is theatre. Imaginary, created by artists. We observe everything so we can duplicate it later, even the blooming of a flower."

"That flower creation was wonderful," said Pavel.

"Yes, that was wonderful. Wasn't it?" Prochazka smiled at the memory.

Pavel was off in a corner of the workshop carving the foot of a particularly complicated life-size rod- and wire-controlled marionette that would be an addition to a production of *The Tempest*. He was behind schedule. The workshop was very busy that day. Several costumers worked at a fevered pace pinning costume pieces on the few live actors employed by the theatre, who were all in various stages of undress in the area reserved for costumes and fittings. The other craftsman were putting last minute touches on props and puppets, while prop masters fitted finished clothing over the puppets that were ready to go. The workshop always seemed to be teeming with people right before the opening of a new play. The energy in the room crackled. Everyone was focused on their work when Prochazka burst through the door.

"Everyone! Come to the stage!"

The people in the workshop regarded one another. This was unusual, since there was so little time before opening, and Prochazka made it his custom to leave everyone alone to finish their part.

"Come on. There is little time. Everyone!"

Pavel followed his fellow theatre folk out of the workshop, down the alley and into the ground-level entrance to the theatre, where Prochazka was busy guiding people into seats. Some sat on the floor. Nina was already in the theatre, her face flushed, excited. Pavel gave her a questioning glance, and she put her finger to her lips to motion him to be quiet. Pavel had no idea what was going on. What he did know was that Prochazka and Nina had been working on something at the kitchen table for about two weeks, talking about it well into the night, and that she kept folding and refolding what appeared to be a large piece of very stiff, painted cloth.

"Ready?" asked Prochazka.

"Ready," said Nina.

Prochazka got up on the stage, opened one of the trapdoors that led to the area beneath the stage, walked down the steps and shut the trapdoor behind him. There was silence, followed by what sounded like very rapid breathing coming from below the stage. Pavel and his fellows from the workshop scanned each other's expressions, searching for a clue as to what unusual thing was to occur.

Without warning, a thing was growing, a stalk-like object, green in color, from the floor of the stage, through a hole no one had noticed. As it reached its full height, almost two meters tall, it opened out at the top in a burst of red and gold and purple, and leaves popped out from the sides of the stalk. Prochazka and Nina had created a magnificent and enormous flower that could "grow" from the floor of the stage.

Thunderous applause and shouts erupted from the workers, and Nina cried. Pavel was astounded. The sound of something metal against metal was heard from below the stage and the flower shifted a bit, then held in place. Prochazka emerged back through the trapdoor, bathed in sweat, holding a huge bellows in his hand. He had used the air from the bellows to inflate the flower that Nina had folded and refolded over weeks, in a precise and deliberate manner that would enable the cloth to unfurl onstage like the perfect and beautiful blooming creation it was.

"And *that*, my dear colleagues, is the magic of theatre. You have all worked very hard. Nina and I wish to show all of you our appreciation for your efforts to create the magic of this theatre. Our gift to you. Good show tonight!"

Pavel never loved his parents more than at that very moment. The flower was never to be seen by the audience and was a one-time performance. Prochazka meant it when he said it was a gift for the people who made theatre happen.

Prochazka brought Pavel out of his reverie to continue what was becoming a very serious talk with his son, which puzzled Pavel. "The thing is," Prochazka continued, "we are a little like the scientists. We know how things work. We examine them to try to create the illusion of those things later. We don't question their origin in terms of explaining them in any other way than what is rational and what we can see. We know why the seasons change, we know that if someone gets sick that it is the sickness that kills them, not God, or a demon, or a vampire."

"People called me that. Vampire. Demon. Other things," said Pavel.

"We know. We tried to keep you from that as much as we could."

"You have."

Prochazka had a worried expression on his face and rubbed his hands together like he was washing them.

"Nina and I have always been grounded in the real world while we work at creating the imaginary world. It is not the way most people live. Most people live by the Church. You understand this, yes?" Pavel waited for his father to continue. He did not comprehend where the conversation was headed.

"That does not mean that we do not believe in magic, especially when the magic is right in front of us. That magic of course being you, my dear boy."

Prochazka rubbed his hands together with more vigor.

"People prefer the Church," said Pavel who was unsure how to react after being referred to as *magic*.

"That they do. Which is what I came to speak to you about."

"Is something wrong with Máma? Are you saying she is sick?"

Pavel became frightened by the expression on his father's face.

"No more than I. We *should* be sick, after years of breathing sawdust and bits of metal and such. Our lungs have taken a beating, to be sure. You need to be careful about that. You have many years ahead of you, and this workshop and theatre will all be yours."

"You aren't going anywhere."

A serious expression suddenly flooded his father's face.

"Pavel, I need you to listen to me. Do you remember when you were very small and some men came to talk to your mother and me?"

"I remember. You were both crying when they left."

"Yes, well we were crying for a number of reasons."

"You were sad?"

"We were also ecstatic. We could not believe the number of good fortunes we were given that day. Nina and I had no children, and then we were blessed with our own little puppet."

Pavel smiled at the memory.

"Me."

"Yes. You. We were crying because we were happy about that. And those men. The men that came to see us—"

"Who were they?"

"They are business men. They heard you were with us, and they wanted to make sure you were well cared for."

This did not make sense to Pavel.

"Why would business men take an interest in me?"

"It turns out there are a few special people like you in the world, and it is their job to make sure that you are looked after."

"Special people?"

"Well, yes, Pavel, you are special."

"Please. Explain, Táta."

Pavel's heart beat a little faster. Was his father telling him there were other people like Pavel? Other odd people who did not grow?

"They set up our family with a business affairs firm in town to look after all our affairs and to make sure that the theatre, workshop and land were all paid for. When they did that, Nina and I thought we'd go head over heels. We were not doing well, and we were afraid we would lose the theatre. I did not know such businesses existed, but they do. They said they would make other investments for us over time, so that when the time came, you would be able to be on your own. They helped us, Pavel. You are, in fact, a very wealthy man."

This last sentence of Prochazka's was incomprehensible to Pavel.

"What?"

"Yes. A wealthy young man. But you are still very much a child, Pavel. You are not like others your age. Perhaps that is our fault."

Pavel tried to unravel the meaning behind everything his father said to him.

Prochazka continued. "It is time that we meet with the business affairs office. Together. I have gone by myself over the years, but you will have to take care of everything now. I have signed over the ownership of the theatre and workshop to you. I will not be here forever. All the paperwork is in order, and you are protected."

Prochazka went to the wall of Pavel's room where there were pegs for coats and hats. He gave both a coat and hat to Pavel.

"But—"

"No 'buts,' my puppet. This is the way things are done. It is a very modern way of doing things, these men tell me. I want to make sure the theatre does not get sold and turned into a dry goods store with a brothel at the back."

"Táta!" cried Pavel.

"Oh, I agree, there might be a very high need for that sort of thing, you know, a pound of flour, a sack of oats and a fuck—"

"Táta!" Pavel laughed.

Prochazka laughed with him.

"But I would prefer it remain a theatre. Give me something to haunt after I'm gone, yes? You are quite an artist, you know. I taught you what I know, but you have taken that skill much further than I could have hoped. The master now learns from the apprentice."

Pavel knew there was something his father was not telling him.

"So. You were crying because you were happy."

"Yes."

"No other reason? Were they able to tell you anything about me? If these men look after people… like me, they must have some information."

Prochazka did not meet his eye, which was an unusual thing for the large man to do.

"Yes. That was the day when we were introduced to much that could not be explained. We never spoke of it with you."

"No."

"You are not angry with us for that, are you?" asked Prochazka.

"I could never be angry with you, Táta, but I would hope for honesty."

His father looked uncomfortable, worried. Pavel had never seen him in this state. The large man who feared nothing, suddenly seemed more than a little frightened.

"It is important that you do not get angry," said his father.

"You said these men looked after people like me—were *they* like me?" Pavel's heart beat a little faster.

"They were like you."

"They were escaped puppets?"

Pavel inspected Prochazka's face, so earnest and serious.

"Ah yes, my escaped puppet with his clipped strings. I'm afraid I lied about that."

Pavel smiled, relaxing a bit. "Of course you did. All men lie when it comes to talking about escaped puppets. You taught me that. You might be shocked to know that I am also aware there is no Sankt Nikolaus."

Prochazka smiled at his son.

"That I did."

Pavel thought about the scars on his shoulders. "So. These men. Let us call them escaped puppets for now. Did *these* men have clipped strings?"

"I did not see them." Prochazka sighed.

At that moment, Nina stepped into the doorway.

"Máma. You are both so serious today. What can I do?"

Nina began to weep, and sat down on the end of the bed, clutching a portion of the blanket that she proceeded to knead in her shaking hands as a sort of worry cloth.

"Darling, all you need to know is that we were blessed when you were brought to us, as those men explained. You brought us hope. As they said you would."

Pavel had many questions but knew he would have to wait for answers, at least for now. He put on the coat and hat handed to him by his father.

"I wish to meet these men," Pavel said to Prochazka.

"They are expecting us."

Pavel and Prochazka walked to the town. The streets were crowded with people who brushed past the two men as they walked, side by side. Pavel was oblivious to everyone, lost in thought. People had no faces that day; as if he were walking past hundreds of moving oil paintings, thick brush strokes that revealed outlines and color and the stones of the street below his feet, basics of people's clothing, but the faces were blurred, making everyone anonymous or interchangeable with anyone else. He was too excited and too focused on the people he was *about* to meet to have any interest in the hundreds of people going about their activities. He tried to concentrate on everything his father had told him. The theatre was his! And whoever he was, or wherever he had come from, he had people looking after him. They in turn had taken care of Nina and Prochazka, for which he would thank them.

In town, tucked into a large row of stone buildings

flanking a dusty cobblestone street, was a door that led to a basement room.

Trope & Co. was etched into the door glass. A simple sign. An unremarkable door, inconspicuous to passersby.

Pavel turned the handle on the door and found it locked. He turned to Prochazka.

"They are expecting us?" Pavel asked.

At that moment the door was unlocked from the inside, and it opened inward to a modest entry. A tall man stood right inside. He wore expensive clothing and shoes, and Pavel noticed also the heavy leather gloves upon his hands, almost like the work gloves he and Prochazka used in the workshop. The thick, rough gloves were very out of place with both the surroundings and the clothing worn by the man who seemed a gentleman of means. What was odder to Pavel was how very ordinary the man looked. He was tall, but not so tall that he would stand out or above a crowd. His age was indiscernible. He could have been in his twenties as easily as his fifties; it was impossible to tell. His facial features were so ordinary that if Pavel were to be asked to describe him later, he would not be able to, as if Mr. Trope wore some sort of unnatural mask, making it impossible for Pavel to discern his real face. When Mr. Trope spoke, however, his voice caused Pavel to start. The man had a voice that conjured a picture of a weasel in Pavel's head. Scratchy, high pitched, with a certain condescending lilt to each word. Pavel did not like him.

"Please come in. My name is Leonard Trope. I'm very pleased to meet you at last, Mr. Trusnik." Mr. Trope reached out his gloved hand and shook Pavel's own. Pavel took in the surroundings and gazed at Prochazka who smiled back at him in assurance. Mr. Trope motioned for Pavel to sit in a chair on one side of a large, darkly stained oak desk.

"My father tells me he has business with you. Business about me? I was not told until today."

Mr. Trope went to a sideboard against the wall and poured tea from a silver set. He held up the sugar bowl and creamer to Pavel who indicated yes to both. He handed Pavel a cup of tea and sat down, continuing to explain the business in his high-pitched rasp. Prochazka stood, looking unsure of himself and curling his hat between his hands.

"Mr. Prochazka, would you be offended if young Mr. Trusnik and I spoke alone for a little while?" Another man with the same nondescript features entered the room from the corridor. He carried a tray of sandwiches and tea. Pavel tried to get a glimpse of the man's eyes, but the man kept his head down. Pavel noticed that he too, wore heavy gloves.

"Mr. Prochazka," said the man who'd entered, "If you would do me the kindness of accompanying me for tea, I was about to have it in the library room. Do you mind? There are sandwiches."

"That would be very nice." Prochazka winked at Pavel as he left.

The men exited, and Pavel sipped the sweet and milky tea. It was delicious. He raised his eyes to Mr. Trope, who watched his reaction to the tea.

"Bergamot. That's what gives the tea that flavor you are enjoying. I had a feeling you might like it. An herb that you can grow yourself one day. Dry the flowers and add it to the tea. I'll send some home with you if you like."

Pavel took another sip. "Thank you."

Mr. Trope continued, picking up his own cup of tea

and holding it between his gloved hands.

"It was not our intention, nor your father's, to keep anything from you, but rather a question of timing. We did meet one time. You were very small. You may remember there were some men that came to the house when you first arrived?"

Pavel was surprised. He did remember the men, but he did not think it possible that Mr. Trope could have been one of them. It had been so long ago. Pavel did the math in his head. If this man was like Pavel and was stunted and took a long time to grow...

"Ah, yes, you are trying to figure out how old I must be, yes? How old is a grown man, do you know?" asked Mr. Trope. Pavel noticed for the first time that the man's eyes had pupils which swirled with the same blue to red to amber and back to blue that were visible in Pavel's own eyes when he saw his reflection in the glass.

"Are we related?" asked Pavel.

"No, we are not," said the man. Pavel was glad to hear that. Something about Mr. Trope bothered him a great deal.

"You have a library room?" asked Pavel.

"Yes. Hundreds, no, let me make a correction, thousands of books. Do you have an interest in books?"

"Very much."

Pavel tried to imagine what a library with thousands of books might look like in this strange, tucked away store front. He imagined passages and corridors lined with bookshelves. Pavel surveyed the office. Dark wood, dark rugs... a heaviness and strength showed in everything that furnished the room, including the well-crafted furniture. Mr. Trope sat behind a heavy oak desk, facing Pavel.

"Prochazka tells me you have no formal education."

"I was taught to read and write by Prochazka and Nina."

"What about other languages? French, Italian, German?"

"Well, of course we speak German. We have to, for the theatre, though puppet theatre allows many performances in Czech. Italian and French, no I'm afraid not. Nor English."

Pavel was not sure why Mr. Trope would be interested in how many languages he was able to speak.

"What about your interests. Do you have any interest in learning anything beyond the art of stage craft? Science? Mathematics? Engineering? The medical arts?"

Pavel felt no desire to educate the weasel-voiced man before him on the use of math and engineering that went into stage craft. He did have a desire to learn much more, however, and the idea of the library Mr. Trope spoke of intrigued him.

"All of it interests me. I read books. I learn much from them. I would be grateful to borrow a few from your library. I promise I would take care of them."

Mr. Trope inhaled a wheezy breath and rasped out another question.

"So you prefer to be self-taught?"

"I like staying close to the theatre and to Prochazka and Nina."

"They are getting old, aren't they?"

Mr. Trope's words cut Pavel. He had been watching Prochazka and Nina grow old, and he was afraid of being left alone without them. He could not imagine a world without them in it. "And I am not. Getting old. Is that what you were going to say?" Pavel asked. "That I don't wish to be away from them in case—"

"They leave you? Yes. I was going to say something like that."

"My mind is as obvious as that?" asked Pavel. He breathed to calm himself. He concentrated on the smell of the room, the tea, the bergamot flowers that gave it that delicious taste, the musty smell of papers and books, a slight mildew that came from a tapestry hanging on the wall. After he breathed in the various scents in the room, feeling a bit more relaxed, he brought his attention back to Mr. Trope, who had been looking at him in a curious manner from across the desk.

"You have learned to take calming breaths when you are feeling uncomfortable?" Mr. Trope asked. Pavel felt as if his mind was being intruded upon.

"Prochazka and Nina taught me. It is an old theatre trick used by actors. To concentrate."

Mr. Trope smiled and brought his tea back to his lips to take a sip. Pavel noticed his lips were quite thin which added to the rodent-like nature of the man. Pavel focused his gaze upon those lips. Mr. Trope placed his teacup back down on the desk. Pavel marveled at the delicacy with which he handled the teacup in such bulky gloves.

"Why do you wear gloves?" asked Pavel.

Mr. Trope did not answer. He continued instead with the topic at hand.

"Prochazka and Nina have lived long, healthy lives and are in their seventies. They have lived longer than most people around us. Most people die when they are much younger, after a short life filled with hard labor that breaks the body. Your parents have not suffered from disease or even an accident. So many things can destroy a body before it has a chance to get old. Their long life is due, in part, to the fact that perhaps they are happy. Happy people tend to live longer. We think you have helped make them happy, Pavel."

"But?" Pavel asked. He did not appreciate the condescending tone Mr. Trope had when talking about Prochazka and Nina. He sounded like he was referring to them as pets.

"Time is a funny thing. For a man like you, time tends to move in a very rapid manner; days go by in a mere flash. Years to us are what days must seem like to other people. It must seem like yesterday that you first arrived on the doorstep of Prochazka and Nina, and yet here they are, old, gray, soon to leave this Earth."

Pavel started breathing again, concentrating on the objects in the room. He focused on a globe in the corner and tried to make out various locations. He was about to get angry, and his parents always told him he was not allowed to get angry. He did not want to let Prochazka down today. He chose his next words with care.

"I would prefer that you not speak of my father and mother like that."

Mr. Trope put up a gloved hand and made some sort of gurgling noise in the back of his throat that Pavel guessed was supposed to be some sort of reassuring sigh, but the sound sickened Pavel.

"How old are you, Pavel?"

Pavel did not know the exact day or year of his birth,

but he tended not to think about his age. Prochazka and Nina had never talked about it with him, other than to say that he was "stunted."

"Time does not move quite the same way for you, does it? Still feel like a young boy? A mere lad in his teens?"

"I suppose. Why am I like this?"

"Perhaps that book reading of yours would allow you some answers? The study of the physics of time, perhaps?"

Pavel had no idea what the man was getting to and was eager for Mr. Trope to explain everything to him. Mr. Trope, however, parsed out information in a slow and deliberate manner, as if he were handing Pavel individual pebbles with a pair of tweezers, one by one, stopping after each to take a sip of his tea while wearing his gigantic gloves.

"The what?"

"Never mind. I get ahead of myself sometimes," Trope said. Pavel thought that last claim was ridiculous. The man had told him nothing, let alone gotten ahead of himself. "Well, to answer your earlier request, you are more than welcome to come here, whenever you are not busy in your workshop, and help yourself to any of the books here. We have every available subject for the person who prefers to be self-taught. History, language, art, music, even the erotic arts." Mr. Trope put an odd emphasis on his last words which he followed with a short, high-pitched, giggle.

Pavel cleared his throat. "Indeed," he said, shifting in his seat, uncomfortable.

"Whether at home or in formal university or in *many* different academies or universities over time, people who live as long as you do may as well become educated on a variety of subjects. Languages, for example. You will more than likely not be doing theatre and making puppets fifty years from now."

Pavel's curiosity was piqued. "You said something about people who live as long as I do. How long is that?"

Mr. Trope did not give a direct answer, a habit Pavel was finding increasingly annoying.

"You did not tell me your age," Mr. Trope said. "I will say it. You are thirty-nine. What do *you* tell people?"

Prochazka and Nina had long ago advised Pavel against mentioning his age to others.

"I do not mention my age to the people I meet. It may alarm them."

"But of course. Look at you. You appear to be the age of a young lover who has yet to meet his future bride." Mr. Trope made the high giggling noise again. Pavel felt as if Mr. Trope was taunting him.

"I beg your pardon?"

The mention of a bride started a tiny seed in Pavel's mind, to grow and irritate and crowd out other thoughts. What was Trope up to? At that moment, Trope switched subjects and slid an inkwell over to Pavel and handed him a quill.

Mr. Trope cleared his throat. "Would you like to take care of the matter of the paperwork before we continue our conversation? It is rather pressing that the pesky business of money be out of the way. There are deeds to add your name to, properties to transfer."

"Properties?" asked Pavel, his mind still on Trope's mention of a "future bride."

"Yes, Mr. Trusnik. In addition to the theatre, adjoining workshop and residential house, there are other properties that we took the liberty of investing in for you over the past thirty years or so. With care and with deliberation, we made a purchase every few years, so as not to draw attention. We will continue to do so, of course, and will, with the proper preparation, venture further abroad with your investments than here in Prague. You own this very building, for example."

"What?" Pavel was stunned, because the building seemed enormous. Mr. Trope laughed a wheezy and phlegmatic laugh in response to the look of surprise on Pavel's face.

"Oh, not the entirety of the structure that lines the street. You can go outside and see where structure meets structure by different architectural hand. No, only this building, but I assure you, there are several businesses and dwellings within that provide a modest, yet significant source of income."

Pavel was stunned. Prochazka, by all modern standards, was the financial equivalent of an aristocrat. Over the course of the next hour, Mr. Trope brought out paper after paper, to which he added his name or transferred into his name. By the end of the hour, on paper at least, Pavel, like his adopted father, was one of the wealthier people in the entire city. Only in the event of the death of both Prochazka and Nina would all ownership be transferred to Pavel Trusnik.

Mr. Trope took the quill away from Pavel and lay it upon a blotting rag on his desk. "There. It is done. We are very pleased that our little firm may be of assistance to you. Do you have any further questions?"

Pavel had one question that had been nagging at him from the moment Mr. Trope had mentioned it, and it had stolen his focus during the entire business portion of the signing of the documents.

"You called me "a young lover who has yet to meet his future bride.""

"Ah. Yes. Love. One day you wish to fall in love. You will wish to marry, is that it? But you are already thirty-nine and that has not happened. Why are you thus concerned?"

"I would like to think it possible, if I met the right person and if she would have me."

Mr. Trope's eyes with the odd and swirling pupils fixed on Pavel. His expression became quite serious. "You and others like you were born different. The oldest of your kind that I have met is four hundred years old. But our lifespan potential might be longer than that. We do not know. We *do* know that we don't live forever." Mr. Trope made a show of examining his gloved hands.

"That is impossible," said Pavel.

"I assure you that it is not."

"What you are saying is insane," insisted Pavel.

"Beliefs and facts are beginning to get confusing, aren't they? You see yourself in the mirror every day, Pavel. What do you think?" Pavel did not know how to answer this man. He accepted what Prochazka and Nina told him and everyone else. That he was stunted. He accepted that was reality.

"Tell me. What do you know about art?" asked Mr. Trope.

Pavel was getting impatient with Mr. Trope. He seemed to keep changing the topic, or choosing roundabout ways of getting to the point. Pavel's annoyance grew, and he shifted again in his seat, crossing one leg over the other as he answered Mr. Trope with a shortness that revealed his impatience.

"Not much. I like some of it well enough."

Mr. Trope rubbed his gloved hands back and forth over one another.

"Have you ever heard of a Putto?" Pavel had no idea to what Mr. Trope was referring, but that feeling of being taunted returned to him.

"I admit to toying with you about mention of the erotic arts, young love and marriage," Trope continued. "I suppose I wanted to see how you would react. My hope was that you would be one who is unaffected by the subjects. How regrettable that I was wrong, and for that I'm sorry."

Pavel felt his face flush. Mr. Trope had admitted to toying with him. About love. He sat, waiting for him to finish.

"You may not fall in love, Pavel. Your kind cannot marry. You cannot engage in the erotic arts."

Pavel felt himself getting upset and he started his rhythmic breathing again, the way his parents had taught him, concentrating on the grain of the oak desk in front of him, the worn spot on the rug below his feet, the rug pattern itself of unicorns running among trees, surrounded by small winged children. An odd pattern for a floor rug, more appropriate to a tapestry, he thought. He allowed his focus to return to Mr. Trope, who had continued speaking, his tone quite serious. It sounded as if Mr. Trope was issuing an order.

"Not only is it dangerous, but it is forbidden. Consider yourself informed. You are not, under any circumstances, to engage in any act of physical love with another. The consequences of that are quite severe."

Pavel stared at the horrible man. First Mr. Trope told him his parents would die soon, then he told him he could never love or marry. According to Mr. Trope, Pavel was to live for countless years. Alone? The idea was impossible to grasp. Mr. Trope continued.

"Some of your kind join the Church. We suggested that as a possibility to your parents." Pavel realized why Nina was crying that morning and why Prochazka was talking about the Church.

"More as a way of discretion, I should suppose," said Trope. "As you experienced yourself as a boy, people like us can often draw the attention of others even when attempting to avoid it. Someone who never gets sick? Who stays young? These people are often fodder for religious hysteria or superstition. Where better to avoid that than within the walls of a church? You can travel from congregation to congregation every decade or so."

Pavel succeeded in controlling his breathing enough that he felt he could respond.

"I can assure you, I have no intention of joining the Church."

"No, I suppose you would not," said Trope.

Pavel gestured his hand around the office where they sat.

"What about you?" asked Pavel. "Is this your 'monastic' existence? Handling the business affairs and acquiring wealth for others like us?"

"Yes, I suppose it is."

"And how old are you, if I may ask," said Pavel.

"Two hundred fifty-seven on my last birthday, though

the date of my birth is questionable. My mother died in childbirth and there are no relatives who lived much longer after I was born who could tell me when that exact date was." The sound of Mr. Trope's high giggle following that statement seemed to tear a hole straight through Pavel's head.

Pavel's face felt quite hot again, and his breath came in short, staccato inhalations that did not produce enough air. He did not feel well at all. Mr. Trope went to a basin on the counter and wet a cloth which he handed Pavel.

"I'm sorry," Mr. Trope said as he laid the cloth upon Pavel's brow.

"I feel sick," said Pavel. Trope reached out a gloved hand and placed it on Pavel's shoulder in a calming gesture and held it there until Pavel's breathing slowed to a normal rate. Pavel concentrated on a spot upon the floor, but he had too many thoughts running through his head as his pulse raced. Fear and adrenaline coursed through his veins as he became overwhelmed with the information he was hearing from Mr. Trope.

"These meetings never go without leaving our clients feeling a little sick over the knowledge that they are so very different from their fellows. The financial stability does not seem to lessen that."

"We cannot have children?" asked Pavel once his breath returned to a more regular rhythm.

"I am very sorry Pavel, but that cannot happen. We have made arrangements that you will want for nothing. You have wealth and property.

"What if I don't believe you? What if I wish to marry someone, and we choose to have children?" asked Pavel.

"You may not sire children, Pavel. There is great risk."

Trope's voice was firm.

"What happens?" asked Pavel.

"What do you mean what happens?"

"If I sire children. You mean the mother will die in childbirth, like mine did? Did I have a father who is like me?"

Trope shook his head. "The mother will not live long enough to get pregnant, let alone give you a child."

Mr. Trope went back over to the basin and wet the cloth again, brought it to Pavel and handed it to him. Pavel took it and dabbed at both his face and neck; however, he kept missing the area he intended to apply the cloth, the blood pumping through his ears and head causing him to be distracted and clumsy. He felt anxious and wanted to leave the room, so he stood and paced. Mr. Trope walked to the door and opened it. A large man with red hair entered the room and stood by the door.

"This is McGovern," said Mr. Trope. "He is here to moderate our meeting, should we have need of that."

Pavel considered the large man, then turned his attention back to Mr. Trope and continued his pacing over the odd floor rug. Mr. Trope went back to his place behind the desk.

"You were born to normal mortal people who lived normal mortal lifespans. What happened to your mother was tragic, albeit common. In your father's case, his life was cut short by the plague. That is the story we adhere to, although in your heart, I believe you know better."

Pavel's eyes teared, and he wiped his hand across his face.

"Mortal people."

Mr. Trope placed his gloved hands on the desk and spread his fingers.

"We are neither mortal, nor immortal. We can be killed. We can kill ourselves. We can die of old age. We do die, eventually."

A thought began to form in Pavel's head.

"The gloves. Do you wear the gloves to protect your hands, or are you protecting others from your touch?"

Mr. Trope got up from the desk again, moved to a cabinet on the wall, opened it and removed two pairs of gloves identical to the ones he was wearing. He handed them to Pavel.

"These are for you. We do recommend that you wear them when around other people."

Pavel examined the gloves, then put them in his lap, unsure what else to do with them.

"What about homosexuals? They do not have children, yet they couple. I am aware of this. I have met many who have come through the theatre over the years. Are there homosexuals of my kind?"

"Yes. And their circumstances are the same as yours— you are asking for yourself?" Pavel shook his head. "No, they may not couple. People of your kind, whether homosexual or not, cannot make love because they cannot, for want of a better term, enter another. Become one. There are no exceptions."

"Explain this to me. What are we? Please be honest. No euphemisms, no hints, no more wheezy giggling."

Mr. Trope's face grew still at the obvious insult, then his expression changed to one of resignation.

"Your parents led me to believe you were a likeable

young man. Far more grown up than you appear to be today. You are actually quite immature, aren't you? And it appears you have a vindictive streak in you, don't you. Maybe you are a bully?"

Pavel knew he had gone too far. His father was in the other room and would be disappointed. Worse, Pavel would not get any further information if he was rude to this man.

"I am sorry. That was rude of me," said Pavel.

Mr. Trope coughed once and motioned for Pavel to drink more of his tea.

"Why do I have scars on my back?" asked Pavel.

"Pavel, I have to explain these things in a kind of order. There is a—"

"Why do I have scars on my back? Was there something there that was removed when I was born?"

"As I was saying, there is an order to how we explain these things to our clients. We can't start anywhere and have things make sense."

"I repeat. Why do I have scars on my back?" Pavel raised his voice. "What was removed from my shoulders?"

"Mr. Trusnik, I am afraid we have to adjourn our meeting for today. We need you to be calm when we give you all the information."

Pavel reached across the desk and in one move, grabbed the lapel of Mr. Trope's jacket and dragged him across the desk, holding him before him. He put his face close to Mr. Trope and in a menacing whisper asked "What *am* I?"

The man called McGovern moved from his place in front of the door to get between Pavel and Mr. Trope. He removed Pavel's hands from Mr. Trope's lapel and, without any effort, moved Pavel to a spot on the other side of the room.

McGovern spoke for the first time. "Please remain calm, Pavel. It is crucial that you remain calm." Pavel backed away from the large man.

"What do you think of the rug you are standing on?" asked Mr. Trope, who seemed unmoved by being attacked. His lack of reaction made Pavel even more furious. His frustration led to the sudden fear that he was here to be removed from his parents, which led to sudden rage, and Pavel lunged again at Mr. Trope. McGovern barely got to him in time to hold him back. Mr. Trope backed away and answered the question.

"They were wings," said Mr. Trope.

"*What?*"

"You were born with wings. They were removed at birth by the midwife."

"Wings? Like a bird?"

"Yes."

Pavel snorted and pulled his arms away from McGovern's grasp. "Did they have *feathers*."

"First you insulted me. Now you are mocking me. I asked you if you had heard of a Putto. Or Putti, if we're to use the plural. They are pictured in the rug you are now standing on."

Pavel looked down at the winged children dancing among the unicorns and shook his head. "This is preposterous."

"I assure you, everything we have discussed today is true, as preposterous as it sounds, to use your word."

"What is a Putto? You aren't going to tell me that I'm

an *angel*. A mythical creature? Like the unicorn? I may not believe in a God, but if there was one, they would not create something like me. No one could be that cruel. This is more likely some sort of deformity, like a sixth finger, or a tail or a missing arm."

"A deformity does not allow you to live for hundreds of years, Pavel," said Trope.

Mr. Trope made a slight wave with one hand at McGovern who moved back toward the door and stood at attention.

"An *angel?*" Pavel stood, mouth agape, uncomprehending.

"Perhaps. There are so many different stories. Myths. Legends. What we know is that, for whatever reason, something inherent in our nature brings a feeling of hope to people. We feel the same deep amount of hope within ourselves, and that hope provides in us a certain measure of optimism in our fellows. It keeps us from… well, from becoming destructive, which we have a great capacity for. I will get to that. Think about the hope you brought to Prochazka and Nina. They despaired before you arrived at their door. The cruel other side to bringing hope is that we cannot touch those people. They get sick. They die."

Pavel got up to leave. He stopped and turned to Mr. Trope. McGovern adjusted his position in front of the door.

"I am some sort of angel of *death*, then, is that what you are saying?"

"We don't like to think of ourselves that way. So dark, so sad. We call ourselves Putti. A term in the art world given to winged children who possess great passion."

Pavel pointed at the carpet. "Like Cupid?" he asked,

skepticism dripping from his voice.

Mr. Trope released a phlegmatic sigh. "I don't expect you to accept this today."

"Are there no women born like this?"

Mr. Trope shook his head. "Sadly, not that we have found, but that does not mean it has not happened. It means that they have not survived."

"Survived?" asked Pavel."

Mr. Trope completed a wheezy sigh and continued, though he seemed to have tired of their meeting, and of Pavel.

"Mr. Trusnik, I assure you we have thought of this. You must understand that the world of men has not been kind to the fairer sex. Nor has it been kind to *anyone* perceived to be different, and therefore misunderstood. People have been burned at the stake for having green eyes. Or that extra finger you mentioned. Or a mole in the wrong location on their body. If there were women who were born like you, and it is possible and very likely there may have been, they were probably put to death at birth. Many of the boys have been. You were to be put in a bag and drowned in the river. But that did not happen."

Pavel blinked, his breathing starting to get rapid again. He felt a stitch in his chest from the flow of anxiety. "What am I supposed to do?"

Mr. Trope tried to speak in a soothing manner, but the wheezing and raspy quality of his voice brought further anxiety to Pavel.

"Continue bringing hope to people. Your theatre is a very good place for you, now that I consider it more carefully. I suppose the theatre is a church of its own variety.

Audiences go there to congregate between the walls of the theatre and wait for the show, all possessing a desire to be uplifted, transformed, or to escape. You fulfill that hope, in a brilliant and magical way, year after year. I have been to shows in your theatre, and they are quite good. That is what you can do. And perhaps, with your new financial circumstances, I have given you a little hope as well, yes?"

"I have read my Greek mythology, Mr. Trope. *Hope* is the virtue that was left behind, cowering in the corner of a box, shut up and forgotten after Pandora released everything *else* into the world. What you have given me today is not hope. You have given me money. And disappointing advice. That is all."

Mr. Trope moved back around the desk to face Pavel and motioned to McGovern.

"Your emotions are in a heightened state and I am afraid you will have to remain our guest a while longer until you are calm again. Your passion could bring about unfortunate consequences for the people outside in the street if you were to leave here angry. "Mr. McGovern, will you please ask Mr. Peters and Mr. Prochazka to come in here a moment."

Pavel was again enraged. "You cannot keep me here!"

Mr. Trope spread his hands before him. "Yes, I assure you that we can. It will be for the best. You can amuse yourself in our library. Very soothing."

Prochazka entered the room with the man whom he had accompanied to tea, Mr. Peters. Prochazka had a worried expression on his face.

"Pavel?" he said.

"Pavel will be staying with us for a few days, while he

adjusts to all the information we gave him today. I feel it may have overwhelmed him."

Pavel started to lunge for the door, but McGovern and Peters grabbed hold of him and held him back.

"Táta!" yelled Pavel. He managed to break away from both men and attempted to hug his father. Prochazka, frightened, stepped away from his son.

"Táta?" A realization came to Pavel at that moment. Everything came to him in blinding and sudden clarity. Táta would not touch him. Something in that moment struck him, and he looked down and noticed his clothing, as if for the first time. He wore all hand-me-downs, from other people. Nothing ever fitted or tailored to his body. No mother or seamstress had ever touched him with a piece of cloth or measuring tape. His parents were, according to Mr. Trope, quite well-to-do, but his clothes were cast-offs. His entire life coming to the fore of his brain, Pavel realized that he had never been touched, hugged, kissed or embraced in any way, by anyone. Most importantly, neither of his parents had ever held their son. And now his father backed away from him in fear. Pavel felt his heart breaking.

Chapter 10

1720

"Wake up, my little puppet." Nina stood over Pavel's bed in the workshop, smiling at him. She made a little motion with her hands that mimed what a puppeteer would do when controlling a marionette to hug another marionette or person. This motion was how Prochazka and Nina expressed their affection for Pavel, instead of hugging or kissing him.

Pavel remembered the first time they started the game that became the family's normal way of expressing love for one another. He had arrived, afraid of beatings or of being touched. Prochazka had told him that they would honor his wishes, though Nina seemed reluctant. He remembered that three men had come to their home and that after they came, his parents stopped trying to pat him or hug him or kiss him or any of the things his adopted mother first tried. Prochazka had patted him on the back on one occasion, that being when he first arrived, but never again after the three men had come to visit. His mother had cried after they left.

Sammy the Redheaded Weird Boy was the name given to Pavel's first puppet and the marionette who Pavel trained with until he was ready to master the others in the workshop. Pavel remembered Prochazka showing him how to work the controls until he could make the odd looking puppet work perfectly on his own. Prochazka always taught him by picking up one of the other marionettes in the workshop and using that as an example, instructing Pavel to watch with great concentration and to then copy Prochazka. In this way, Prochazka taught Pavel how to hug.

"Here, Pavel. Watch me, then you do it." Prochazka had moved his fingers and hands in a motion that caused his puppet to make a hugging motion. He then walked the puppet over to Pavel's puppet and used the motion to hug Pavel's puppet. The boy laughed.

"There now, you see? I'm going to put the puppet down and make the motion with my hands and then I want you to do it." Pavel watched as Prochazka set down the marionette on the bench, then turned to Pavel and made the exact motion in the air that he had made when there had been a marionette in his hands.

"Now you do it." Pavel watched Prochazka do it again, and the man and boy repeated the action several times until Prochazka said that it was perfect.

"When Nina and I do this, we are saying we love you, and we are hugging you, our little escaped puppet. If you feel like it, this is how you can hug us back. Okay? This way we can respect your wishes and still hug you when you're a good boy, all right?"

Pavel faced the floor, unsure. Nina walked into the workshop.

"Darling, look what I have taught our boy."

"And what is that?" asked Nina.

Prochazka showed Nina the hand motion. Nina and Pavel joined in, and after trying the motion several times they all laughed. Nina's blue eyes shone.

"Looks like I get to hug my puppet after all," she said.

Pavel thought about that as Nina stood over his bed, waking him. He sat at the edge of the bed and Nina sat down beside him.

"I've got a big breakfast ready for you. Get washed up and come out to the kitchen."

"I have been thinking," Pavel said.

"Have you? And what have you been thinking about?" Nina asked.

"I have been thinking that it would be okay if you hugged me. For real," said Pavel.

Nina's expression turned from startled to sad in a mere instant. Pavel didn't know what he had said that was wrong. He tried to reassure her.

"I won't mind anymore."

Nina made the motion with her hands again, as she had done for years, burst into tears and left Pavel's room. Pavel, confused, washed up and headed to the main house and let himself into the kitchen where Prochazka sat, head in his hands. He could hear Nina's sobs coming from behind the bedroom door.

"What's wrong with Máma?"

"Oh, puppet. Nina is at an age where women feel many emotions about many things, sometimes happy, sometimes sad. Sometimes she cries even if she's happy or laughs when she is sad. It often does not make much sense. She is having a day like that."

Pavel contemplated what his father had said and responded. "Do people lie about other people?" he asked.

"What?"

"The way they lie about escaped puppets. They always lie when talking about escaped puppets. But do they lie about people?"

"Well, of course I *might* be lying," Prochazka said. "Everyone in theatre lies." Prochazka put his face back into his hands.

Pavel never again brought up the subject, nor did he ever attempt to hug either of his parents.

Pavel's memory came to him in Mr. Trope's office as he stared in horror at the look of anguish on his father's face, and he was flooded with a full and sudden understanding. He began to weep.

"Mr. Prochazka, I think it is best if you leave now. We will send the young man along in a few days."

Prochazka's cheeks were wet with tears, and he mumbled an unintelligible reply, turned around and left the office. His father, always larger than life to Pavel, suddenly appeared very small. Small, broken, and unhappy.

Pavel felt alone. Angry, hurt, but most of all, completely alone.

Chapter 11

1859

The years following the inevitable loss of his parents produced in Pavel an extended period of creation and focus upon the theatre which he now ran. Pavel's grief at losing his family sparked a period of manic energy that he used to develop projects and inventions, new engineering feats, and exciting, highly advanced puppet designs. He became rather the equivalent of the mad scientist, his behavior becoming eccentric, and the employees and actors of the theatre who came and went, were more than happy to leave him alone to his activities unless they had a question about a specific item needed for a production. He continued to control the puppets in various performances and would perform their voices, but he did not interact with the other puppeteers that he had trained, or the live actors. He became a virtual hermit, venturing out on those occasions that required his presence elsewhere. Interaction with others was contained to the theatre and theatre craft. Industry and invention became his focus, and when he was not in the theatre or adjoining workshop, he was in the library at Trope & Co., reading every book he could get his hands on in every area: language, science, engineering, architecture, literature, religion, art, medicine, and alchemy. There was no subject that Pavel did not devour in his studies. If he required another book, he asked Mr. Trope to acquire it for him. During those occasions when he came to the offices to use the library, Pavel noticed that Mr. Trope appeared to observe him constantly, from a distance, but never engaged him in conversation unless necessary, nor invited him to dine. He left him alone. Everyone left him alone.

During his period of solitude, Pavel used the knowledge he had acquired from some of the books to develop various herbal concoctions that he ingested, experimenting with anything that might have a mind-altering effect. He experimented with a number of highly poisonous plants, flowers and mushrooms, using tiny quantities, in various combinations. He tested foxglove, wormwood, water-hemlock, cow parsnip, petunia or anything else from the nightshade family, and morning glory. He had an endless variety of beautiful and volatile plants available to him, if he went looking, with which he could experiment. He found his preference was for those combinations that increased his wakefulness while producing a slight hallucinatory effect of a shimmering halo around everything that met his gaze.

Decades went by with Pavel unaware of the passing of

time. His theatre thrived season after season, both critically and financially. On rare occasions, someone from Mr. Trope's office would come by with a bundle of clothing for Pavel that was in the current fashion. He did not seem to notice such things and would grab anything available in the theatre or workshop when dressing himself, even old costumes. For someone who appeared to be so youthful, he had taken on the personality of an aging eccentric, though his increasing use of mind-altering concoctions made his behavior somewhat erratic and more similar to that of an immature child than an aging eccentric. He made no friends in the theatre with any of the multitudes of craftsman or actors that had crossed the threshold over the years, even those who stayed beyond a few seasons. He taught the various craftsman in his workshop who came and went how to better create their illusions, how to make grander and more fantastic marionettes, how to design lighting for greatest visual effect, all the while wearing his protective gloves given him years before, at his first meeting with Mr. Trope.

The two did not like each other, but they carved out a civil relationship, since they were resigned to dealing with one another for many more decades than they had already. While Pavel was busy focusing on theatre and reading and concentrating on his next invention or illusion or recreational herbal medicine, a full century passed him by. A century of virtual isolation. The fact that there were actual people coming and going in Pavel's world was the one thing keeping him from being left in complete solitude, so it had not gone unnoticed that he was becoming more than an eccentric. There was talk that Pavel might be a little mad and rumors of his use of herbal intoxicants ran rampant. Further gossip stated the drugs were making him lose his memory, and in truth, he did often forget his lines during performances. The audience rarely noticed the omissions, but his fellow theatre cohorts were distressed. He was no longer the nice, likeable young boy that had slept in a cot in the theatre when Prochazka and Nina were alive. It was therefore alarming and a little unnerving when Pavel rushed through the door of Trope & Co. with over-animated enthusiasm on a particular day in 1859, more than one hundred years since Pavel and Mr. Trope first met.

"Mr. Trope! You must see this!" Pavel burst through the door of the offices of Trope & Co.

"You can't—" cried a young man in the foyer.

"Oh, but I can. I'm a *special* client! Didn't they tell you about their escaped puppet?" Pavel's swirling pupils were dilated. The man, alarmed, attempted to stop Pavel as he ran down the corridor, past the library, to Leonard Trope's office. Pavel rushed inside, slamming the door behind him.

"Trope!" he said and shook the gloved hand of the startled man behind the desk.

Pavel moved from one foot to the other and back again as Mr. Trope appeared to be scrutinizing him. Pavel wore what appeared to be a portion of a jester costume, composed of yellow and green triangles of silk fabric with small bells stitched to the hem. Pavel combined the ridiculous costume with an outdated dinner jacket. The fabric of the jester costume was thin and clingy, making it obvious he was not wearing any undergarments. The clothes carried with them a slight odor of cat urine. Pavel was not wearing the clothing that Trope & Co. delivered to him, and the stubble on Pavel's chin and his strong body odor suggested he'd not bathed or shaved in quite some time

"Mr. Trusnik, to what do we owe the pleasure?" asked Leonard Trope, his own strange pupils swirling, his voice wheezing, raspy. How Pavel loathed Mr. Trope.

"I have an investment to make. I want you to attend to it." Beads of sweat popped out all over Pavel's forehead and his hands had a small tremor.

"We would be happy to handle whatever it is. We would, of course, run an investigation to determine if this investment is in the—."

"Best interest, yes, yes, yes, I'm familiar with the speech. Tell me, did you get the gift I sent you?" Pavel's rapid speech had a staccato edge to it, and one of the beads of sweat broke free and trickled down his brow.

"If you mean the painting, yes we did. It was kind of you, thank you," said Mr. Trope.

"Did you find it intriguing, sad, uplifting, melancholy? There are such a variety of emotions one experiences when looking at a piece of art, that one scarcely knows where to begin in describing them. Which was it for you? Which? Hmm?"

"Mr. Trusnik, I believe you are toying with me, somewhat. And you appear to be under the influence of something. Are you?" Pavel made a noise that sounded like something between a laugh and a snort as he paced the room, the smell of cat urine wafting off of him as he moved.

The painting to which Pavel referred, by an artist named Francesco Guardi, was entitled *Allegory of Hope*. The background of the painting depicted a peasant woman on the shore of a body of water carrying what appeared to be a basket of wheat. One stalk of wheat blew out of the basket. In the foreground, dragging himself across the ground toward the woman, or the wheat, and carrying what might be a log for a fire, or a portion of a pillar from some ruined building, or perhaps dragging himself over debris lying about on the shore, was a young child with small wings sprouting from his shoulders. The woman faced away from the cherub, who would more likely be referred to in art circles of the day as a 'putti,' the secular and profane expression of non-religious passion and what people like Pavel, according to Mr. Trope, indeed were. Emphasis on the "profane" if Mr. Trope could be believed, thought Pavel, though he did not believe a shred of it and had read almost every book in Trope & Co.'s library in an effort to refute Trope's claim.

"Well, Mr. Trope, I believe that the painting represents many things. I arranged to have it purchased on the anniversary of the death of my parents. I could think of no better place for it to hang but in your offices. You have done so much for our family."

"Are you mocking me, Mr. Trusnik?"

"Not at all. I believe you told me, would you believe over *one hundred years ago*, that what you do here at Trope & Co. is *hope*. Hope. Rhymes with Trope. Coincidence? So I bought you a painting that sums up to me what *hope* is. *Hope* means being ignored while I drag myself toward some futile ideal, my longing or passion having no end. Perhaps I should throw a bag over my head, jump in the river and drown, to get it all over with. The painting is so bleak, as if I commissioned it myself, but we know that's impossible. Do you think this too literal an interpretation? I'm afraid I was never formally schooled, so my observations are rather pedestrian, to say the least."

Mr. Trope sighed, or what could be considered a sigh escaped him, though the exhalation of air more resembled air being squeezed out of a broken bellows—high, whistling, gurgling.

"You are lonely," said Trope.

"That's what you gleaned from all of my dripping sarcasm and expensive gifts inspired by bitterness and mockery? I'm *lonely*? You, Mr. Trope, are a veritable genius."

Mr. Trope ignored the young man's rudeness.

"It has been your choice to remain at the theatre and in the workshop which seemed to agree with you. It is, however, unnecessary, and apparently your solitary lifestyle is doing you more harm than good. People do move on, enjoy different lives for themselves, take up new professions, travel, meet new people, et cetera. You have the means to do all of these things, yet you have chosen to stay here and live in a theatre workshop."

"My family is here."

"Your family died over one hundred years ago."

"Prochazka's bones still rattle in the theatre," said Pavel.

"You can't be one of those people that believes in ghosts and that the theatre is haunted by your father."

"I believe his bones still rattle around the theatre."

Mr. Trope considered this statement.

"We can take care of human obstacles that endanger you. We can make sure you are financially comfortable, and we can even arrange new identities, new homes, travel and adventure. We can make every attempt to clothe and feed you if that is what you need, and judging from your attire today, we need to pay more attention to that. We can do all of this. What we cannot do is remove your bitterness or your loneliness. I'm sorry, Mr. Trusnik, but directing your anger at us will not satisfy you. You chose to stay in one place with limited experiences to stimulate you, other than the books in our library...."

Mr. McGovern entered the room without speaking and stood by the door. Pavel watched as Mr. Trope shot McGovern a look. Mr. McGovern made a slight bow, and exited the office.

"Yes, yes, I understand. I apologize if I have offended," said Pavel. "One hundred forty-five years I have been at the theatre—a mere fraction of those years involved having a family. The theatre family is so fickle and transient, one cannot rely on it for any type of comfort, can one? Can one? Really? Especially if one never becomes intimately involved with anyone else, yes?"

"Mr. Trusnik, I—"

More sweat made its way in rivulets down Pavel's forehead, and he wiped at it with the sleeve of his dinner jacket.

"And I appreciate the use of the books in your library that you have let me help myself to over those years. I have learned much. So very much. And yes. Yes, the theatre does agree with me. But I am here about something else. Have you seen this book? It is new. It was difficult to acquire a copy, but I managed. It is in English."

Leonard Trope picked up the book. The title read: *On the Origin of Species by Means of Natural Selection, or the Preservation of Favoured Races in the Struggle for Life*, written by a scientist named Charles Darwin.

"I have not heard of it, I'm afraid," said Trope.

"I don't believe you. You are a horrible liar. Is there any one thing you tell the truth about? There is not a thing published or talked about, supposed about, no new religion or superstition or rumor or piece of gossip about any of *us* that this office doesn't hear about or know about first."

"This is a book about natural selection of the species. Evolution," said Trope.

"Exactly! At long last, someone with brains has come up with something that might explain people like us. This accident of nature that stands before you might have an actual, scientific explanation, one that might even turn out to be quite simple. We may be like one of the moths with the spots he talks about. I blend in with my environment, and none of those nasty natural predators affect me, like disease, or aging, or my head exploding in my sleep—"

Mr. Trope started to interrupt, but Pavel cut him off. "Better yet, if he is right, then does it not stand to reason that there are other men and women like us? In the great balance of nature and natural selection? If we are to live such a very long time, it does not make sense for our survival to be what it is, if there are no others."

"Mr. Trusnik, I am afraid I must ask you again. Have you ingested anything today that would make you intoxicated in any way? You are unnaturally animated."

Pavel snorted. "Unnaturally animated. I would think *all* of us are unnaturally animated, wouldn't you agree?"

Mr. Trope could not hide his annoyance. "I am simply saying that if you are in any way intoxicated, that it might be a good idea to stay with us a bit until it is out of your system. We wouldn't want you drawing unnecessary attention to yourself, yes? Your pupils are quite dilated. Very noticeable. And the unusual nature of our eyes is something we do not wish to draw attention to. In your current state that is impossible."

Pavel bobbed his head vigorously up and down, like a mechanical doll. He paced the room. Mr. Trope took that to mean agreement.

"Mr. Trusnik, there are very few of us, and it is *because* we upset the natural order of things that there are so few. We are an anomaly."

"There are a lot of paintings of us if we are such an anomaly," Pavel said. "Everywhere. Babies with wings, babies with horrid looks on their faces like those of a demon, or angelic faces of those that bring joy and light and love into the world. Tell me, was it babies like us who modeled for those paintings?"

"Perhaps the earliest ones were inspired by our kind. That is before my time. Later, it became something akin to myth or religion, and reality was no longer at play. I have been told in the early times, the wings were considered a blessing of some kind. A sign of fortune. The babies were allowed to keep their wings."

"What happened?"

"People died, of course. Do you listen to anything? And then people got frightened. It was the *natural order* of things."

"I want you to invest in the scientist, Darwin. Give him money for more research. I want to give him the opportunity to find out more. That is the investment I wish to make today."

"I see," said Mr. Trope.

"And don't look so worried. I have no intention of making myself known to this man, nor do I have any plans to meet him in person though that is my desire. I wish to ask him any number of questions, but I realize that is impossible. I am not stupid, Mr. Trope."

Mr. Trope shook his head at Pavel. "No, you are not stupid. You are immature and dangerous."

"Well, that is encouraging," said Pavel.

"I have to set up an anonymous foundation for financial gifts, and the money, of course, must come from a bank in England, but yes, that can be done. For a time. It cannot be done in perpetuity."

"But others will continue his study and his research!"

"And the churches will do everything they can to stop that from happening. Pay attention to your own history of experiences. We must be careful. Even anonymous investors get unearthed by those who do not share their worldview."

"Please do it." Pavel picked up the book. "And enjoy the painting!" He burst back through the doorway with the same frenetic energy that had carried him inside.

Pavel rushed back to his workshop, ignoring the looks of the people in the street who gave him wide berth, or the shopkeepers that closed their doors upon his passing. Upon entering the workshop, Pavel went straight to the cupboard over the stove to search for various tea tins, but all of them were empty! The various craftsmen and seamstresses in the shop bent their heads, hard at work on their next production, and did not look at Pavel.

"Pavel."

Pavel whipped around. Mr. McGovern sat in a chair at the table used for meals.

"Did you do this?" Pavel shook an empty tea tin.

Mr. McGovern took notice of the others in the workshop who had dared to look up at the two men. He waved at them.

"Please take off the rest of the day," said McGovern, and all the workers exited the shop.

Pavel was incredulous. "You can't do that!"

McGovern said nothing, but picked up Pavel, threw him over his shoulder, and while Pavel kicked at him like a trapped animal, McGovern carried him into the lavatory and put him, clothing and all, into the bathtub. Pavel had engineered a pump which connected a series of pipes to the outside well, and water flowed through the pipes into the basin, which then ran into the bathtub. McGovern pumped the well handle until water began to flow freely from the spout. He put Pavel's head under the spout where the water proceeded to rush over the back of his head and neck. McGovern held him there, Pavel yelling and sputtering the entire time. McGovern was too strong for Pavel's struggling, and after what seemed an interminable length of time, Pavel gave in and succumbed to the forced bath, allowing the water to continue rushing over his head. McGovern held him there for some time. After he determined that Pavel was no longer going to fight him, he grabbed the cake of soap and a cloth and proceeded to bathe Pavel with a rough hand.

"You stink, you are wearing ridiculous clothing, and you are obviously intoxicated on *something* you have created here. All these things draw attention to you, which we cannot afford. You are going to clean yourself up."

McGovern continued his rough scrubbing. Pavel was humiliated, and at the moment filled with loathing for McGovern, who scoured Pavel as if he were a flea-ridden dog. After McGovern finished washing Pavel, he made him get out of the clothing, wrapped a large cloth around him and walked him back to his room. He handed him one of the bundles of clothing Trope & Co. had delivered to him and motioned that he get dressed.

"I'm fixing you something to eat. Come to the table when you are dressed," said McGovern.

When Pavel made his way to the table he was starting to feel a little shaky. He had no idea how long he had been taking the herbal concoctions that he had carefully developed in specific dosages and added to his tea, producing his desired effect of euphoria and wakefulness. He had not slept for days as he worked on a new puppet. The carving was intricate and he had no idea how long he had been at it before being distracted by the arrival of his book. That delivery had sent him flying out the door, straight to the offices of Trope & Co.

McGovern placed a sandwich and a cup of black tea in front of him.

"Where did you find the tea?" asked Pavel.

"I brought my own."

Pavel picked at the sandwich, realizing it had been some time since he had eaten. He was famished. He stuffed the sandwich into his mouth and drank the tea, while McGovern sat without speaking, watching him from across the table.

"This is the way things are to be," began McGovern, when Pavel finished and sat back from the table.

"The herbs, the potion, whatever you are taking, stops now. You are to dress yourself with care, in the clothes that we bring you, if you are incapable of selecting acceptable attire. You are going to honor the memory of those wonderful people that raised you and continue to be that son, or I *will* come back here, and I will humiliate you in front of your colleagues again. You have become a spoiled, petulant, insulting and horrid parasite of a man, and you draw attention to us all. Do you understand me?"

Pavel was shocked. He considered what McGovern had said, the first person other than his parents who spoke to him in such a blunt and honest manner. He hugged his arms to his body. His hands still had a slight tremor.

McGovern continued. "This concoction of yours. There is talk it is affecting your memory. We cannot afford to forget who and what we are. I repeat, *do you understand?*"

Pavel, agitated, stood and shifted back and forth on his feet. "I understand. I have one favor to ask of you."

"What is that?" said McGovern.

"Will you come visit for tea?" Pavel pleaded. "It doesn't have to be often. Every once in a while. It could be once a year, even."

McGovern considered Pavel's request and softened a bit.

"Trope was right. This is about being lonely?"

Pavel's eyes teared, and he did not answer. He could only move his head up and down, while continuing his agitated movement. McGovern guided Pavel back into his chair.

"I will come for tea. On occasion. Though I will expect you to have bathed." McGovern smiled at him, his rough exterior softening a small bit.

Pavel put out his hand to shake McGovern's.

"But it will only be for a while. Peters and I are being transferred overseas." McGovern was referring to the other man that Pavel had seen in Mr. Trope's offices.

Pavel opened his mouth in surprise.

"Yes, we have other locations. We are needed in America. New York, for now."

Pavel thought about what Mr. Trope had said to Pavel about traveling. He wondered what it must be like, but he was tied here. His family, his roots. He felt bound to the theatre as if it was a part of him. He envied Mr. McGovern, and a part of him would miss the large, red-headed man that dunked him in a tub. In the meantime, until McGovern left, he would look forward to his visits, visits with someone of his own kind. Almost like family, Pavel thought.

Chapter 12

Present Day

Pavel stood in the kitchen at the counter, and wearing heavy gloves, he worked with a section of wire mesh. He concentrated on connecting the mesh to a strong piece of wire, using needle-nose pliers to do the final twist on the material. His concentration was interrupted by the ringing telephone. He was on every "no-call" list imaginable, and he could not think who would be calling him now. He glanced at the readout on the modern phone on the vintage kitchen countertop. The area code was from the Valley and the prefix familiar, but he could not place it.

"Hello?"

He recognized the stern voice on the other end of the line.

"It's McGovern." Why would he be calling after all this time?

"Is something wrong?"

"Word has come to us that you may be in need of assistance with a matter of some delicacy."

"Are you speaking of the letter I received from Trope regarding someone accessing the blueprints to my home?"

"Indeed. When do you expect your visitor?"

Pavel sighed. His privacy since the time he broke the Great Rule was rather an illusion. They knew about the visitor. McGovern had a way of inserting himself into Pavel's life. Though contact was rare, and there was no socializing for Pavel per the terms of his current arrangement, McGovern and the others like him kept tabs on the lives of certain individuals and offered assistance in times of great need or when the potential for exposure was imminent. Recent events warranted their involvement.

"I am capable of addressing the issue."

"There was an incident north of here a while back. A family. Violent. Troubling."

Pavel considered this. A thousand images flooded his head, his theatrical imagination working overtime.

"That sounds dreadful."

"Yes. It is. It is not an isolated incident. Our investigators have revealed some things that are alarming, to say the least."

"Have you spoken to the police?"

"We are working out the best way of informing the proper authorities without drawing unnecessary attention, of course."

McGovern's information gave Pavel a burst of

renewed energy, and he was anxious to get off the phone so he could finish his preparations.

"I have prepared for the situation, I assure you."

"We have every reason to believe that very same person has targeted your home."

Pavel was growing more impatient but tried to keep his voice neutral when speaking to McGovern.

"Yes, I am aware. I received the letter about the blueprints. I have been watching the subject of your concern. And I have taken every precaution."

"The unstable are very unpredictable, Mr. Trusnik."

You have no idea, Pavel thought. Being left alone with no social contact for seventy years had taken a toll on his own stability.

"So are old theatre rats, McGovern." Pavel smiled for the first time in a long time. "I believe it has been too long since I have put on a show. Don't you?"

"Will you be attempting to contact Mr. Lamb, then?"

Mr. Lamb. A name Pavel had not heard in a very long time. He answered, choosing his words with care before speaking.

"I was told contact was forbidden. You know that. I have had no contact with any of you, and I have not seen my dear friend in a very long time. I would have no idea how to reach him now."

There was silence at the other end of the phone. It was obvious to Pavel that McGovern did not believe him.

"Strange. We have not heard from Mr. Lamb, either, in quite a few decades. We had reason to believe that he might try to get in contact with you or that he may have travelled to see you. When did you see him last?"

Pavel thought how best to answer.

"Are you telling me that Mr. Lamb is missing? How is that possible?"

McGovern sighed over the phone. Pavel continued.

"It has been too long to remember. Prague? I think when last we spoke he planned on traveling to Corsica. Or perhaps it was Morocco. I can't remember. He does travel the world, though. It is his stage, as he likes to say. I am sure wherever he is, he is being quite entertaining."

"Right. Very well. We wish you good luck." McGovern hung up.

"Yes, indeed. It has been a very long time." Pavel walked back to the workshop and surveyed the many puppets lining the walls, hanging from the ceiling and sitting around like actors waiting backstage for their cue. He approached one cupboard, a floor to ceiling cabinet built into the wall with a lock on the front. He took an antique skeleton key from around his neck and opened the cabinet.

"Hello, my dearest dears. We have not had a proper visit together in such a very long time."

Four large rod- and wire-controlled puppets hung inside. The woodworking of their faces was exquisite. Pavel spoke to each of them in turn. "My Lear, how I have missed you and your counsel. Dear Mother Gertrude, your hugs and laughter. Hello, my beloved Juliet. Not a night goes by that I do not relive every touch, every look, every embrace, every laugh. Ah, Othello. My dearest friend. Such talent. Such perfection for the stage. I miss you. I miss you all. My family. My escaped puppets."

Pavel's puppets that he had tucked away in a locked cabinet, were carved replicas of Prochazka, Nina and his beloved Žophie. The last puppet, the one he called Othello... upon looking at Othello, he felt a pang of tremendous regret and again, he felt something wet upon his face. The poem tugged again at his unreliable memory. *Thursday's child has far to go....*

The detail and structure of the puppet faces had been achieved by taking plaster casts of living peoples' faces to use as templates. Over the years, Pavel had carved and painted each face, away from the prying eyes of other craftsmen in the workshop.

Local legend claimed that even after Prochazka died, his bones still rattled on the stage when the company performed a tragedy. Pavel chuckled at the memory as he unbuttoned the clothing on the puppet which was a perfect replica of his beloved Prochazka.

"I think for tonight's performance, we will give you something less to wear," said Pavel, and he continued to remove the last of the garments on the large marionette. He stood back and admired the restored human skeleton. The bones were ancient.

The bones were Prochazka's.

He removed the puppet from the cabinet and brought it over to the table. He placed his expert fingers under the wood façade that covered the skull and removed the exquisitely carved puppet face, leaving the bleached white skull without ornament.

He studied the bones, all that remained of his adopted father, who had withered and died. How many audiences had continued to enjoy Prochazka, but as a puppet in his own theatre, after Prochazka died? Hundreds. Thousands. He could not be sure. He turned to the marionettes remaining in the cabinet.

"I will be back for you later, my dears." Pavel shut and locked the cabinet and secret crypt.

Before leaving the workroom, Pavel stood and took a good look out the back window at his garden, again breathing deeply upon imaginary scents. Ophelia's distraught speech from *Hamlet* entered his memory as he, from his spot behind the window, inspected the traditional English knot garden he had planted years before.

"There's rosemary, that's for remembrance. Pray you, love, remember. And there is pansies, that's for thoughts. There's fennel for you, and columbines. There's rue for you, and here's some for me; we may call it herb of grace o' Sundays. O, you must wear your rue with a difference. There's a daisy. I would give you some violets, but they withered all when my father died."

Patterned after one of the rugs in his foyer, the knot garden had been planted in an intricate geometric pattern using a dwarf hedge of meticulously trimmed rosemary with various compartments for other herbs, separated by brick, pea gravel and sand. Most of the other herbs were inspired by mention in Shakespeare's plays. The rosemary had been long in need of trimming, the hedge no longer in any discernible pattern and smothering most of the surrounding herbs. In fact, all the herbs had long since flowered, and dead blossoms hung down, in need of dead-heading. The gardeners that came to maintain the yard were under instruction to leave the knot garden alone, for that was Pavel's alone to maintain. A bee flew around the herbs in search of something substantial to collect and soon left. A tiny hummingbird flitted around the dead flowers of the rue. The bird was no bigger than an inch or two in length. Pavel remembered a moment in the back yard years before, when he was watering the garden with a hose, and one such hummingbird hovered in front of him, bathing in the spray from the hose. When had he allowed his garden to become so sloppy and ill-cared for? His precious herbs. Even more precious, his rosemary. *Rosemary, that's for remembrance.*

Chapter 13

1882

"I enjoyed your show," said a woman as Pavel exited the theatre.

Pavel squinted at the slight figure before him, silhouetted by the bright sun.

"Thank you."

"I love the puppet theatre. Did you make them as well?"

"Yes, we make all of them."

"My name is Žofie. I already know your name, Pavel Trusnik."

Pavel made a slight bow. He did not respond for she continued without seeming to take a breath. The tiny woman was quite enthusiastic.

"I'm *fascinated* by puppet theatre. I think that I am quite obsessed. Such work. Such imagination. Such *life* goes into every puppet. The way you make them move! I'd like to see your workshop now, please." She seemed quite determined.

Pavel was somewhat taken aback.

"Aren't you with someone?" he asked. " Do you have a chaperone? You should not be out alone."

"To see puppet theatre? In the afternoon? You must be mad."

Žofie seemed not much more than a girl, sixteen or seventeen, with a glorious mane of auburn hair contained by her sensible bonnet, and bright blue eyes that seemed to twinkle when she gazed up at him. She was very small in stature, with a tiny waist and small shoulders covered by an equally sensible long-sleeved dress in dark wool that cascaded to the pavement, her tiny shoes barely visible, poking out from beneath. He thought she was beautiful. Pavel had managed to avoid much, if any, interaction with people outside of the puppet workshop or theatre for many years, and the longer the woman stood there talking to him, the more uncomfortable he became. His hand shook a little, and he wiped it across his face.

"Oh, dear, I've insulted you," she said.

"No. It is… no."

"Good! Then may I see your workshop now, please?"

He was saved from answering by one of his colleagues. Andrej Cerny, a dark-skinned, handsome young man, came through the stage door behind the theatre. Andrej had joined the theatre within the past couple of years as one of the few live actors. Like most Czech theatres, many plays combined live actors and puppets onstage, though the majority of the acting was done using puppets, to keep costs down

"Pavel, talking to a lady?" Andrej joked.

"And you are the actor, Andrej Cerny," declared Žofie.

Andrej feigned surprise. "You know my work, beautiful lady? I am flattered."

"I can read. You are in the pamphlets. I was attempting to coax your friend here into showing me the workshop where the puppets are made. I am more intrigued by puppets than actors."

Andrej mimed stabbing himself in the heart and threw his body to the ground. He raised one hand to the woman, pleading.

"You cut me to the quick and then you murder me, beautiful lady! But you may make it up to me. Allow me to give you the tour, and I will forgive you." Andrej stood and brushed off his clothes. "Pavel is not so good with these things." Andrej winked at Pavel, who'd remained still and at a loss.

"Now is not a good time. But later. You should have a friend with you? A companion? Your mother, perhaps?" Pavel said.

"I am required to have a chaperone?" said the woman.

"I'm afraid I must insist."

"But I wish to see it *now*."

"That will be impossible."

"If I have to have someone with me to see the workshop, then I will get someone. Will my father be a sufficient chaperone?"

"Why, yes, of course, your father would be fine," Pavel said.

Andrej Cerny smirked at Pavel. "Our Pavel is a very

proper fellow. Yes, bring your father. We love to have more audience at the theatre!"

"I do have to go," said Pavel. "Perhaps tomorrow, following the afternoon show? You can bring your father, and we will go to the workshop after? I can fix us some tea."

"We will be here, Pavel Trusnik. I promise!" Žofie walked away from the two men, raising a parasol over her head to shield her from the afternoon sun, the ruffles of her dress dragging on the dusty ground behind her.

Pavel watched the young woman as she walked down the street. He felt a fluttering in his stomach that was unfamiliar to him, and his face felt hot. He felt a stirring in his groin. He realized Andrej was watching him. The actor smiled.

"'I can fix us some tea'? You are a *very* proper fellow, Pavel Trusnik. Though not so proper, maybe?" Andrej pointed at Pavel's crotch. Pavel did not have to look down to know there was a bulge there. He was embarrassed. Andrej turned his attention to Žofie. "I think some of our puppets might be larger than her," said Andrej. "I prefer a little more meat on a woman. But what would you know about that, proper fellow Pavel?"

"Not much," Pavel said to Andrej.

Andrej laughed and walked away, his gear slung over one shoulder. "See you tonight!"

Pavel gathered his things from the theatre and walked the short distance through the alley back to the workshop to sleep a little before the evening show. As long as he could remember being a part of the workshop, he had kept a bed in the back. People had come and gone over the years. More than one hundred years had passed since Prochazka had died, leaving Pavel with the task of inventing an entire life history that included Prochazka as an ancestor and family patriarch instead of his father. The nomadic world of the theatre artist and constant variety of the audience that came to see the performances had made that an easy task. The initial decades following the death of his parents had been the most difficult, but time, focus and dedication to being part of a puppet theatre made it easy for Pavel to get along in his small world, blending into the workshop. Either he kept to himself, or he hid within the drape of black fabric attached behind the puppets during the performances. He was unremarkable to look at. While not unattractive, he was not someone who stood out or would stay in the mind of people who came through the workshop, whether craftsmen, or actors who wandered from one theatre job to the next. He was plain in appearance and not someone to settle into the mind of an audience member. His hair was neither light, nor dark, his build was moderate, his face was of an average shape and his skin clear of anything that might distinguish him. His eyes were the one thing about him that a person might find interesting, but one had to be quite close in order to see that the pupils had a certain bluish glow to them that could change to deep red or amber and back again to blue. His name was listed in the pamphlets as one of the craftsmen of the theatre, among many others who had crossed through the doors of the workshop over the years. The list included names from the past and the present. Pavel did this in part as cultural pride—a way of displaying the great number of people over the years who helped the theatre prosper and also as a way to further blend into the fabric of the theatre as yet another name among many that had passed through the door on their way to making the type of magic that only a theatre can produce. Prochazka was still listed as the owner and artistic director. Žofie was the first person Pavel had met, since Prochazka, who seemed to not only notice him, but single him out from the others. Pavel found that to be a bit of a mystery, a rather uncomfortable, yet somewhat exciting, mystery. She was quite beautiful, not to mention a bit strange, and Pavel looked forward to meeting her with her father on the morrow.

Pavel had difficulty sleeping during his afternoon rest period. After tossing around, unable to get comfortable, Pavel left his room for the workshop area and its wood-burning stove which he had added years ago. He put on a kettle for tea and wandered around, inspecting the various pieces in progress. He examined an unfinished carving of a donkey head that would be used later that year for a production of *A Midsummer Night's Dream*. He picked up a chisel to make a small adjustment around one of the eyes.

"Are you Pavel Trusnik?" said a man's voice from the doorway.

Pavel turned around to see a tall, angular man of about forty, in expensive attire.

"I am. Is there something I may do for you?"

"You met my daughter, Žofie, earlier today."

Pavel was a bit startled. He masked his lack of comfort by concentrating on the contour of the eye of the puppet he was holding, and continued to work at it with the chisel.

"Ah, yes. Žofie. You are her father? She wanted a tour of the workshop."

The man stepped into the doorway and made a show of looking around the workshop. He walked closer to where

Pavel was working.

"Yes, she has spoken of nothing but that since she arrived home after the theatre today. That and the fact you would not give her a tour. She is quite vocal about that."

"I see."

The man eyed the kettle burning on the wood stove.

"The water is heating. May I offer you some tea?" Pavel asked.

"Yes, thank you."

Pavel put the puppet down on the workbench, rubbed the chisel with a cloth before placing it next to the puppet and moved over to the stove where he began the ritual of putting together a tea for the two men, opening cupboards, bringing out plates, a bag of pastry, forks and spoons. He kept his heavy work gloves on while he put together the tea.

"Žofie tells us that you would not offer her a viewing of your puppet workshop without a chaperone. Is that true?"

"Yes. I meant no insult. I think it is proper that a young lady be accompanied, especially where there are a lot of tools and things lying around."

"And actors."

Pavel eyed the man.

"We do have the occasional actor hanging about the workshop, yes. We fit them for costumes here, and meals are often taken here during rehearsal periods."

"Well, I wanted to meet this young fellow from the theatre that did not act like a fellow from the theatre."

Pavel was annoyed with the man. Too often, people felt the need to openly insult people of the theatre as if doing so was not only acceptable, but somehow expected.

"I see. Well, not all people from the theatre are

charlatans, rogues, gypsies and prostitutes, sir. Though I'm well aware of our reputation," Pavel said. "Have you come to insult me in my place of business?"

The man appeared to consider his words before speaking again. "My apologies," he said.

"May I know the name of the man I am speaking to, sir?" said Pavel.

"Yes, of course. Forgive me. I am Eduard Rychtar." Pavel had heard of the man. He poured the tea and motioned to the nearby table. They sat.

"I know who you are. The judge. You are quite a powerful man. You humble me by coming to my shop."

"Well."

"Please forgive me if I seemed over-sensitive. People of the theatre seem to carry a certain reputation with them that I find ill deserved."

"No need to apologize; I realize I may have been quite insulting."

Pavel placed a plate of pastry on the table.

"Yes, well. Pleased to make your acquaintance, Mister Rychtar. It is an honor to have you here."

The two men sat, drinking their tea, regarding one another.

"I think my curiosity got the best of me. I very much wanted to meet the man who would dare to say no to my daughter. That is a difficult thing to accomplish with any degree of success," said Rychtar.

"They do seem to hold the true leadership, sir."

"Excuse me? Who are we speaking of?"

"You said you had never met anyone capable of saying no to your daughter."

Rychtar raised his hands in a resigned manner. Pavel continued.

"It has been my observation, after years in the theatre, that even Shakespeare failed when writing of women's complexity. Women do seem to hold the true power, leaving us speechless and in constant confusion wondering how to behave around them."

Rychtar picked up a piece of pastry and appeared to be studying it, then put it down.

"You believe this? Women hold true power? Some would find that a rather weak point of view, coming from a man."

Pavel considered that for a moment and smiled.

"Perhaps I am ahead of my time. Or I have read too many plays." He shrugged.

"Have you have never been married?"

"I have never been so blessed, sir, no. That does not mean that I have not made certain observations over time."

The judge laughed. "I think I might see what has my daughter in such a state of chaos over you, Mr. Trusnik."

"I beg your pardon?"

Eduard Rychtar did not respond to his question. "The theatre is yours? And the workshop?"

"And the adjoining living quarters on the other side. The theatre is a family business, started by the founder of the theatre."

"Prochazka. You are a descendant of his?"

Pavel began his century-old explanation of the theatre, which included the fabrication where he included himself as a distant relative.

"Yes. Prochazka's theatre has been a part of our

national Czech culture for 150 years now."

Mister Rychtar chuckled. "I believe you have started the tour."

Pavel made a small smile. "I suppose it is habit, when someone new comes who is curious."

"I hear Prochazka's ghost still haunts the theatre."

Pavel gave another small smile and got up from the table and moved over to a workbench where he picked up a small marionette, about the length of Pavel's arm, made up to look like a skeleton. He held it up for Mr. Rychtar to see. He rattled it to make a sound as if small bones were clattering against each other. In actuality, they sounded more like wind chimes than bones, since the marionette was made of a soft pine wood.

"So the actors tell me on occasion. They say 'His bones still rattle on stage whenever we perform a tragedy.' Perhaps he decided to stay."

"You believe in ghosts?"

Pavel put the marionette back down on the workbench. "I believe in strong memories. And Prochazka did so love the tragedies."

"You talk as if you knew him."

"No, he is long passed from us, but I have had the privilege of reading his many journals."

"And your parents, are they in the family business as well?"

Pavel did not enjoy being interrogated. No one had been this direct with him in terms of asking pointed questions about his father Prochazka or the theatre. Theatre people or audience members tended to talk about Prochazka like a legendary figure, and few asked Pavel about him. Why would they? To anyone around, Pavel was far too young to have had a personal acquaintance with the man. Prochazka and Nina had been his parents and he had no other family, unless you counted his business association with Trope & Co., so he was unaccustomed to fielding questions about a non-existent set of parents who might have lived in the last decade or so.

"My parents are no longer living, sir. I run it myself."

"Ah. Žophie's mother is no longer with us."

Pavel bowed his head in sympathy.

"I'm sorry."

"You are unmarried?"

"You asked me that."

"Yes, of course I did, forgive me."

"As I said, yes, sir. I am unmarried."

"Any siblings?"

Pavel made a decision to end the afternoon interrogation. He had to prepare for a performance. He inhaled the smell of the sawdust, leather, wool, and metal dust that surrounded him into his nostrils, using the scent to focus upon remaining calm, unruffled.

"You ask a great deal of questions, Mr. Rychtar, that have very little to do with puppets."

"Not part of the tour?" the judge asked. "I suppose not. I was curious. Such an old theatre, such a part of the culture, as you say. An institution. If you have no family, who will take over when you are no longer in charge?"

Pavel suddenly understood of the purpose of the probing questions regarding his family, his business, and his property. Mr. Rychtar was being a father, interviewing a potential suitor for his daughter. The idea relaxed Pavel.

"Ah. I see. If you are asking about the ownership of property, yes, the theatre and land is now mine. I plan on being here for a long time, but I will make the appropriate plans when the time comes. It will, depending on how things turn out, become a theatre of the state."

"A state theatre. How grand!"

"I do not know. Perhaps I will leave it to one of my *actors*." Pavel smiled.

Mr. Rychtar smiled back. "I deserved that." He looked around the shop and back at Pavel. "Well, it was nice to meet you, Mr. Trusnik. I should think I would like to stop by again with my daughter to take a look at how the puppet theatre works in more detail. Would tomorrow be all right? I believe you told my daughter that tomorrow was fine."

"Yes, tomorrow it is. I will make another tea."

"Until then." Mister Rychtar left.

Pavel thought Rychtar was strange, and he was unsettled by the entire encounter, though he understood its purpose. He was not used to having to answer so many questions about himself. He was surrounded by actors and performers who were far more interested in themselves or their craft to probe into Pavel's life or history. He squinted at the table clock and realized he had very little time to get to the theatre for the evening performance. He grabbed a pastry left over from the tea with Mr. Rychtar and stuffed it into his mouth as he ran out the door, down the alley and up the stairs to the theatre's backstage area. That evening, the company would perform *Faust*, an audience favorite due to the scary puppets and high drama. Once backstage, he donned his blacks, the black clothing worn by the puppeteers, and picked up the first marionette he would be controlling and voicing. He had done his part of the performance hundreds of times, but for some reason he was having trouble remembering the order of scenes. That made him chuckle, something he had not done in years, not since he'd been with Prochazka. He wished the man was there now, so he could tell him about Žofie and her very strange father. Prochazka would have liked such a tale.

"Spirits, Witches, Gods, insanity, murder, oh! She goes mad—a poodle turning into Mephistopheles—how did you do that with the puppets? So fluid! So without effort, oh! So much *life* to the play! The man and the demon, wise man versus the fool—so much for the theatre to fill, to do…. It was *breathtaking*!" Žophie raved about *Faust*, which she had seen performed the previous evening.

"I must say, the imagination that went into everything was rather impressive," said Eduard Rychtar, Žophie's father. As promised, they had come to visit the workshop in between shows.

"I wish I had known you were going to attend. I would have made arrangements for your seating," said Pavel. The young woman surprised him in her enthusiasm. He was a little worried about her father. He set out a tray for them at the table which was often used by the theatre people for meals taken throughout the workday, when the actors came in for their costume fittings or when seamstresses and other workers needed a repast. The table was built from a huge piece of alder wood, a much stronger and harder wood than the pine used for the puppets. The table was scarred from nearly two hundred years of use, but it had been constructed by Prochazka when he was alive and had been built to withstand anything. Pavel used this simple, yet sturdy table as an example to himself and to any other workman in the shop of the importance of attention to detail and quality of craftsmanship in anything constructed in the workshop. He had a plate of sliced apple, pastries and open-faced sandwiches which he set down while he moved about the space, collecting cups and things for tea from the cupboards over the stove. The kettle was heating.

"Our seats were wonderful. The play was wonderful!" said Žophie.

"I'm afraid my daughter is quite taken by the theatre. I have horrible fears of her running away to become an actress. I am hoping you might discourage her from this?" said her father. Pavel was unsure whether he was being serious or not.

"I would discourage *anyone* from choosing the theatre as a profession," Pavel said with a smile. "The pay is horrible, the hours are quite long, and do not forget, if people do not like what they see, they throw rotting vegetables in your face. Not very subtle of them, would you agree?"

"Oh dear, has that happened to you?" asked Žophie.

"Not to me, no. Though we have had performances where it did happen. I am either standing behind the puppets or controlling them from the rafters above the stage. I believe it was a puppet named Vincent that was on the receiving end of an overripe tomato on one particular evening, while I was tucked behind him. Thanks to Vincent, I came to no harm." Žophie laughed, eyes dancing. Pavel found he enjoyed making her laugh. He was unused to speaking much to people in such an intimate setting—intimate to Pavel, anyway. His infrequent visits with Mr.

McGovern, where they sat at this very table for tea, had ended when McGovern had travelled to America. How many years was that now? Socializing with McGovern had helped, however, so Pavel was not completely awkward in the presence of others when the situation arose, like now. But it was a struggle. He was at relative ease when he voiced the puppets, draped in black, unseen behind or above them as he concentrated on their control and movement. He was confident when he had to instruct craftsman on the construction of a puppet or a theatre prop, on the best way to carve an eye socket or attach an arm on one of the puppets. He was confident when instructing a crew member how to tighten a hanging scrim, that finely woven cloth used for creating visual effects on stage with lighting, or how best to execute a particular effect the director might want, like fire or the illusion of water on stage. Actors tended to stick together and did not often speak with the people on the more technical side of things unless they had a specific question. Pavel was one of those people, though his puppetmaster abilities were unsurpassed, and he was considered to be more of a craftsman than a performer. Actors did not often speak to him. Further, he made it a rule to not accompany the actors when they socialized. Rather, he did not interact or socialize with *anyone*, other than to discuss theatre craft with other professionals. Pavel kept to himself. Prochazka and Nina had taught him that was the best way to avoid personal questions which could be difficult or awkward to answer.

For some reason, however, he found himself quite comfortable discussing the theatre and talking about his work with Žophie and her father.

"Are you a religious man, Pavel?" asked Rychtar.

Pavel was no longer comfortable. He most hated this type of question.

"Táta, don't ask that."

"If you're asking because of the content of the play," Pavel said, "I think the theatrics and drama of the psychology expressed in the play are what draws theatre people to perform it, not to mention audiences to see it, not necessarily the religious aspects, though those are there, without question. The fascination with the pull between good and evil is undeniable and something everyone can feel on a personal level. There is such a richness and complexity to everyone, don't you think?"

"I would have to agree with that, yes," said Rychtar.

"Oh, will you show me the puppets now?" said Žophie.

"My daughter is rather impulsive. Please forgive her interruption."

"Not at all. If you have had enough to eat, I can show you the shop."

"Yes, please!" Žophie said.

Pavel led the way as they got up from the table.

"I must ask you to be careful where you step. We keep a very tidy workshop, but things can still drop to the ground that could cause injury if stepped upon. I checked everything earlier and did a thorough sweeping, so all should be well, but I still wish to caution you, since we are walking around wood and glass and sharp tools. We'll move around the outer edge of the room and work our way in, all right?"

Žophie moved to follow Pavel's lead. Her father joined them. Pavel picked up a pair of work gloves from a bench and put them on. He moved to an odd little marionette, hanging from the wall, with bright red hair made of yarn and an off-center, clownish expression on its face.

"This is Sammy the Redheaded Weird Boy. My first puppet, given to me as a child. He taught me everything I know."

"He seems quite old," said Rychtar.

"What kind of name is that?" said Žophie.

"Well, look at him. I should think that would explain it. He is a horrible actor and never ended up in any of the shows, but he was a good teacher. And yes, he is quite old, but he can still walk." Pavel took Sammy down from the wall and used the control to manipulate Sammy into walking around the workshop with the others. The top of Sammy's head reached just under Pavel's knee, so Pavel stooped over a little to work the control. Žophie laughed and clapped her hands.

"Oh, that's wonderful! Can you show me?"

Pavel became uncomfortable and was not sure how to respond. He had not anticipated this part of the tour.

"As I said, my daughter is impulsive," said Rychtar.

"Hmmm. I had not planned on a lesson today. Let's see. All right, follow me." Pavel led them by walking Sammy to the other side of the shop where a small marionette of a donkey lay upon a workbench. The white donkey was covered with black spots, and its huge, red-lipped grin revealed large teeth. The puppet's silly expression was due to eyes carved wide, with off-center pupils.

"This is Lucky," said Pavel, picking up the marionette.

"Lucky, the donkey?" Žophie asked.

"What? Donkeys cannot be lucky, they must only be stubborn?" said Pavel. He manipulated the donkey to sit abruptly upon its haunches and to shake its head back and forth, as if it was refusing to move.

Žophie laughed. "All right. Show me what to do."

Rather than guide her hands with his own, the way some puppeteers might teach others, Pavel stuck with Sammy as example. He put Lucky back down on the table.

"Go ahead, pick him up. Use the control, like this." Žophie picked up Lucky and held him, copying Pavel's movements with Sammy. Lucky was small but so was Žophie, and the puppet body reached about mid-thigh level. She had to raise her arms up a bit higher to stretch out the strings that controlled the puppet, but she watched, fascinated, as Pavel showed her in slow motion how to manipulate the strings attached to the control.

"Can you move my hands with yours and show me that way?" she asked, and Pavel glanced at her father, who stood by, observing.

"Žophie, I think you are being a bit familiar. Watch how he holds his own. You can figure it out," said her father.

"I am showing you the way that I was shown. I was taught that it is best to learn it by studying, watching, then doing it yourself from the beginning. Slowly."

"I find that to be true with many things," said Žophie's father.

"Here, watch." Pavel held the control and moved his fingers over the strings as Žophie watched with intense concentration. "This is how we manipulate them."

"Oh! Look! I'm doing it!" Žophie walked the donkey and laughed. Pavel and Eduard both smiled as she proceeded to walk the donkey marionette through the warehouse, improving as she went. She seemed to have forgotten the two men in the workshop and was focused solely on the puppet under her control. Pavel had never seen anyone so filled with happiness, and he remembered the first time he made Sammy walk around the workshop. He and Prochazka had laughed until they thought the very walls of the workshop would come down around them. Pavel smiled at the memory.

"Tell me something, Pavel," said Rychtar, when Žophie was out of earshot, lost in her new activity.

"Yes?"

"Why do you hide that you are, in fact, a very wealthy man who does not have to work and who does not have to live in the back of a puppet theatre workshop?"

Pavel said nothing, and avoided making eye contact with Rychtar.

"I have done a little research on you, since my daughter seems quite suddenly smitten with everything about you and your world. She is like that. She grabs hold of something and never lets go. She is not fickle and does not move from one excitement to another. So I have to look at you with a certain seriousness that other fathers might avoid while their daughters flit from one fancy to the next. It is quite exhausting being this vigilant, because her choices are so permanent. Do we understand each other?"

Pavel did not know how to answer.

"You have done very well for yourself. You own more properties in this town than I do. How did I not know that before my research?"

"I'm not one who likes to stand out in a crowd. Money tends to make that happen to a person if people know about it, don't you think?"

"Ah, yes. There is that aspect to it, yes. I can see a point to desiring anonymity."

"I like my work. I prefer the workshop. I am comfortable here."

"But what if you started a family? What about their comfort?"

"Well, I do not have one, so that has not been a hurdle I have had to jump. I suppose if that were to occur, I would make the changes necessary. Live in a house, perhaps. Get a dog." Pavel smiled at Rychtar.

"For someone who appears to be so young, I think you are quite wise, Pavel Trusnik. Quite wise." Rychtar patted Pavel on the back, and Pavel flinched.

"Oh, I'm sorry. Are you injured?" said Rychtar.

"No, I... no, you surprised me."

Rychtar laughed. "Well, I wasn't going to strike you, young man. Far from that. I must say this has been a very interesting and enjoyable afternoon." Both men turned toward Žophie, who was engrossed in walking the puppet.

"Žophie! We must be going!"

"Oh, dear, must we? I am having such a marvelous time!"

"You may have the puppet. My gift to you for being such an enthusiastic audience and quick student," Pavel said.

"Really?! Oh, Táta, isn't that wonderful? I have a marionette!"

"Yes, dear. Now do you plan on walking it the whole way home?"

"I do!" Žophie laughed.

"Good day, young man," said Rychtar. "We shall speak again, soon."

"I look forward to it," Pavel said.

"As do I!" Žophie ran over to Pavel, placed a light peck upon his cheek and ran back to her father, laughing. "Táta, I have a puppet!"

Pavel stood there, stunned and a little bit frightened as he watched father and daughter walk out the door of the workshop and into the world beyond.

In all of his one hundred seventy-one years, Pavel had never been kissed until that moment.

A voice interrupted Pavel's reflection.

"Are you worried what might happen to her?" The voice came from the doorway. A tall man was silhouetted by the sun behind him.

Pavel realized he still had his gloved hand against his face in the spot where Žophie had kissed him. He dropped his hand.

"I beg your pardon?" asked Pavel. "May I help you?"

"I do hope so," said the man. His voice was rich, deep, like that of a highly trained actor, thought Pavel. When the man walked into the workshop, Pavel was taken aback. The man was African.

"Don't be alarmed. Yes, I am African," said the man, as he walked into the workshop, taking over the space with what theatre people liked to refer to as "enormous presence." He brushed his hand over the scarred tabletop and delicately traced the lace costume on one of the puppets that hung from a wall hook. He turned in a full circle, dancelike, taking in the entire workshop with his gaze, then walked with a confident stride toward Pavel. "My original family called me Cheidu, but for years my name has been Robert Lamb."

"You... are American?" Pavel asked.

"I came from there, yes, but for obvious reasons it seemed best to move elsewhere. But yes, I was born to free parents in the north and educated there. New York, to be precise."

"You are an actor."

"Yes."

"You speak Czech perfectly."

"I also speak German, French, Italian, and of course, English."

"I have never met a—"

"Actor of Colour—to paraphrase how I was referred to in one of my London reviews? I suppose they would call me something more vulgar in America."

"Yes."

"I hear that your program includes a production of Othello?"

"It does. Have you played him?"

"Many, many times. I am quite nimble with a scarf. My hands manage to never make contact with the delicate Desdemona while the cursed scarf does all the work." Robert Lamb began Othello's farewell speech: "*Farewell the plum'd troops and the big wars that make ambition virtue! O, farewell, farewell the neighing steed and the shrill trump, the spirit-stirring drum, th'ear piercing fife, the royal banner, and all quality, pride, pomp, and circumstance of glorious war!*" A lone tear made its way down the face of the actor.

Pavel was moved by the simple and specific emotion that the actor conveyed without effort. "What brings you to this theatre? Why aren't you in London or Germany? There must be many opportunities—"

"For a man of my appearance to play every Moor written for the stage, or to don white face for other great roles—Shylock the Jew, perhaps?" Robert Lamb laughed. Pavel noticed the man's pupils which had a certain bluish glow that seemed to change from deep red to amber and back to blue. Pavel had seen eyes like that before. He knew those eyes well. Trope, McGovern, Pavel himself— all possessed the eyes of the man who stood before him. He felt a sudden anxiousness and wanted to know everything there was to know about this man.

"The puppet theatre is a strange place for a man of your talents."

"There are stranger things. 'There are more things in heaven and earth, Horatio, than are dreamt of in your philosophy.'"

"You have performed Hamlet?" Pavel asked.

"Oh, wouldn't that be the most wonderful thing, to do that?"

Pavel considered that a moment and realized how ridiculous he must sound to the African actor.

"Oh. I'm sorry. Yes, of course. I suppose you would play the gravedigger in that play?"

"And I have!" Robert Lamb chuckled.

"I'm afraid I am without resources to bring a new actor into the theatre. We budget for one, two, sometimes three live actors. Puppets do the rest."

"Can you teach me to act with a puppet?"

Pavel gaped at the celebrated actor. "Why would you want to do that?"

"Why, more opportunities, I suppose. Not fettered by my physical appearance, I could become one with the puppet, powered by my voice, my emotion."

"But payment?"

"Is something we can discuss and not something I am concerned about. But I am afraid I have travelled quite a way and am a bit dusty. Do you have a place where I could wash up a bit?"

"Yes, yes, of course. I'll show you."

Pavel led the strange man to the lavatory and showed him the basin, cloths and soap. The lavatory was not much changed from when Pavel was a child, though the basin had been replaced by a cast iron trough set into the counter, which allowed more room for washing rags and brushes from the workshop.

"I think you'll find everything you need here."

"You are very kind."

"I'll make us some tea."

"You are even kinder," said Robert.

The two men were alone in the workshop, and the actor Robert Lamb did not close the door all the way to the lavatory as he washed. He removed his upper garments to wash his face, neck and torso, and Pavel saw a vast network of crisscrossing scars over the entirety of his back that Pavel surmised to be the result of multiple whippings over an extended period.

Two scars in that map of abuse stood out to Pavel, two scars that had not been made from the wounds inflicted by a whip. Robert Lamb had two bumpy scars that had been stitched by an amateurish hand, one over each shoulder blade, in the exact location as the scars on Pavel's own shoulders.

Pavel gasped.

"I'm sorry. Would you prefer I shut the door?" asked Robert.

"Your scars."

"Yes, over time there have been many people who thought to make an example of me, I'm afraid. Having parents who are free and being educated does not protect one from the slings and arrows of small-minded cowards."

"No. Not those. I am very sorry about those."

"Then?"

"The scars on your shoulders."

"They are as old as I am, and have been a part of me as long as I can remember. I do not remember what made the scars, though I might have an idea or two."

Pavel was shaken by this.

"Yes. You possess the same scars, Pavel Trusnik. I have travelled quite a way to meet you."

Pavel did not know what to make of this. How would this man know anything about Pavel?

"An escaped puppet, finding its way home?" Pavel asked. He realized what he said sounded awkward and weird. The actor studied Pavel.

"I beg your pardon?"

"My father, Prochazka, said that the scars were where they cut off my strings. That I was an escaped puppet that finally found my way home to the theatre."

"Ah! What a wonderful story your father made for you. He must have loved you very much. How old were you?

"Seven."

"He used this story to take away the hurt, the curiosity—"

"The story came to be true. Our whole family became

a type of escaped puppet, I suppose." said Pavel.

"You do know the truth, however?" Robert asked with concern.

Pavel stared at Mr. Lamb and shook his head, as if confused. The years of madness and the use of mind-altering herbs were not so long ago for Pavel that he did not still suffer a certain amount of periodic memory loss. McGovern's visits had been a comfort and companionship, but in the decades of grief following the death of his parents, Pavel's herbal experiments had done a certain amount of damage. McGovern had the frustrating task of reminding Pavel of his reality, though Pavel would turn around and forget much of their conversation by the time their next visit occurred. McGovern told Pavel his mind would heal in time, but Pavel needed constant and vigilant reminders. Together they developed a few tools for Pavel to use to shake himself into reality. Pavel rubbed his thumb and forefinger together, and took a deep breath in an attempt to ground himself.

"My dear man, are you quite mad?" asked Lamb.

"Perhaps. A little. So people tell me. Some also say I'm quite immature." Pavel seemed to feel quite comfortable talking to his new acquaintance. "Don't you find yourself a little mad at times? Aren't you very old? Like I am?"

"My good Mr. Trusnik, I would not be the actor I am without being a raving lunatic. And as to the subject of my age—an actor never reveals his age. Otherwise he may never get to play Hamlet. Or Romeo." His laugh was rich, and Pavel laughed with him.

Several hours had passed since Robert Lamb crossed the

threshold of the puppet theatre workshop. Robert and Pavel sat together at the table, two empty wine bottles between them. The two men were well into their third shared bottle. The actor Andrej Cerny entered and appeared genuinely surprised when he saw the two men. He regarded Robert with a strange expression, as if he did not trust his eyes.

"Andrej Cerny! Meet Robert Lamb, our visiting guest actor from America, by way of London and most recently, Germany," said Pavel.

Mr. Cerny approached the two men with a flabbergasted look on his face.

"I know who you are, Mr. Lamb. I had the great pleasure of seeing you in a performance of *Titus Andronicus* while traveling in Germany with my parents as a boy. I found you to be…"

"Breathtaking?" asked Robert, bursting into laughter. "Not a very happy play for a child, I must say."

"Indeed, but it is one of the reasons I stand before you today," said Cerny.

"Ah, caught the proverbial disease, did you?"

Cerny made a sweeping gesture with his hand up into the air as he bowed to Robert.

"Indeed. And I was going to say that I thought your performance to be chilling. It is a great honor to meet you." Andrej Cerny sat at the table. He appeared to be studying Robert's face.

"You look confused," said Pavel.

"Well, I must say I am, a bit. Why would a celebrated actor come to our little theatre in the middle of nowhere? And how do you know each other? Pavel you are keeping great secrets from us."

Robert poured Cerny a glass of wine.

"Don't worry," said Robert. "I am not here to steal your roles — though I must say I will put up quite a decent fight over the role of Othello when you mount that play next."

"I would not dream of playing that role in your stead. There is always the great villain Iago to play, whom I would throw myself into with complete abandon."

"Ah, Iago. One of our greatest villains," mused Robert.

The three men raised their glasses.

"How *do* you know each other?" asked Cerny.

Pavel took a drink from his glass and responded, "We don't. We only met today!" Robert Lamb snorted.

"I don't understand," said Cerny.

Pavel waved his hand in dismissal.

"Mr. Robert Lamb is to be our guest artist for a bit. As long as he will have us, I think. He'll be staying in the main house," Pavel explained, as Robert protested and rose from the table.

"No, I insist," said Pavel. Robert returned to his seat.

"Well, it is indeed an honor. I must say, Mr. Lamb, you are much younger in appearance than I assumed you would be," said Cerny. The actor had the same odd expression on his face that he had upon seeing Robert Lamb for the first time, part disbelief, part fear.

"Yes, well, the art of theatre makeup is a kind of magic, is it not? I do believe I could still play the ingénue!" He laughed again.

"I was but a child when I first saw you. That must have been over twenty years ago."

"Shush, young man, you are on the very precipice of

revealing your *own* age, which an actor *never* does," warned Robert.

Cerny continued to stare at Robert Lamb as if he was seeing a ghost. Pavel was aware of Cerny's scrutiny of his new guest.

Pavel stood. "I think I better show our new friend to his lodgings. He has travelled a long way, and I'm sure is quite tired."

"Yes, I admit between the travel and the wine, I am quite ready to sleep," said Robert. "Andrej, I am looking forward to our first rehearsal together!"

Andrej bowed again, still looking confused.

"Don't worry, Andrej," Pavel said. "You are still our lead resident actor."

The information did not serve to change the look of confusion on the young actor's face.

"Is something wrong, Andrej?"

"No. It is that… I truly thought he would be much, much older. It can't be possible."

Pavel reassured him. "Well, you were mistaken. Not hard—you know the biographies they give the actors are filled with nonsense. You should know that. You wrote your own!" Pavel laughed.

"Yes, of course. You are right about that. Good night to you, gentlemen!" Andrej drained his glass of wine and left the workshop. The two men exchanged glances as he exited.

"It is unfortunate to be one of us and to be recognizable," said Robert. "But an actor must find his stage."

"You look sad," said Pavel.

"I am. But no matter. Your young Andrej Cerny will

forget about me in no time."

"How will he do that?"

Robert got up from the table and began a stately walk around the room.

"Oh, I believe he will be made an offer by another theatre that will be impossible to refuse. You will need to find yourself another actor like him."

"That should not be hard as there are always more actors than theatres. But how—?"

Robert interrupted Pavel and waved his arm theatrically to indicate the room. "You know what puzzles me, Mr. Trusnik. How on earth have you managed to remain in the same place for such a long time, without drawing attention to yourself? And in a theatre, no less?"

Pavel considered his answer. "I keep to myself, I suppose. I work behind the puppets, not in front of them. People in the theatre are transient. No one remains for any length of time. And in the town? I am not much to look at. I guess I blend in with everyone else."

Robert raised his hand and made a flourishing motion to indicate his approval. "A trait I think you have rehearsed to perfection."

"A little perhaps. I have had no desire to leave."

Robert, a little tipsy, raised his glass again. "You give me a bit of hope, Pavel. Well, that is sort of our job, isn't it?" Robert winked at him.

Pavel raised his own glass. "Hope? In what?"

"That settling down is possible. I am getting so very tired," said Robert.

"Mr. Cerny has recognized you and will have more questions."

"I believe you and I do business with the same firm. Mr. Trope, yes? They do very good work at protecting the interests of people like you and me. I believe they will be able to address the matter of the confused Andrej Cerny."

"I often wonder. Are there so very many of us?"

Robert paused before answering. "I don't know. Wouldn't that be dreadful?"

The two drunk men walked arm and arm out the door, down the alley and around the backside of the building to the entrance of the main house where Robert Lamb, Cheidu to his family and close friends, would be setting up residence.

Robert Lamb, the man who Pavel would also come to refer to as "Cheidu" was about to become Pavel's very first friend, in one hundred seventy years.

"You can sleep here." Pavel showed Robert to his new room, stumbling a little from the effects of the wine.

"Are you sure I'm not putting you out of hearth and home?"

"Not at all. You'll see me in here plenty. We eat here, though sometimes I eat in the workshop if I'm very busy. I sleep in the workshop. I always have."

"I do hope you have refilled the mattress a few times over the past, what, one hundred fifty years?"

The only person who knew Pavel's actual age, was Leonard Trope. He chose to confide in his new friend.

"One hundred seventy. And you?"

"As I said, my dear, an actor never reveals his age." Robert made a show with a flamboyant bow to Pavel, who felt a little betrayed that Robert had not shared the same confidence with him.

Pavel put more wood in the stove to heat the stew that

had been simmering in a pot since morning. He arranged the table while Robert was in the other room putting away his few belongings. Robert returned and surveyed the table.

"A gorgeous meal for two!" said Robert. Pavel raised an eyebrow. "Oh, don't look like that. You are far too old for me, nor do you match in any way the physical ideal that I adore."

Pavel invited Robert to sit. "I was not worried about that," said Pavel "But thank you for your honesty."

"Well, we already share one terrible, deep dark secret, I feel we should be honest. Though I suppose you could tell. About me."

"I would not accuse you of being subtle," said Pavel, smiling. "Or maybe being in a theatre for over one hundred fifty years gives someone like me a certain insight."

"You obviously are not uncomfortable in the company of a homosexual actor, then?"

"Is there a reason that I should? Some new information? You are as you are." Pavel shrugged. "I have watched so many people come through the theatre over the past decades. Everyone has a stripe of their own—some unique tick or idiosyncrasy or proclivity or addiction or *something*." Pavel liked to sit and have a simple conversation with another man. He had not had a conversation like this since he was much younger, and had long talks with his father, Prochazka. He felt comfortable, content. Pavel's visits from McGovern had been brief, civil, but nothing of much substance was discussed, despite all effort on Pavel's part to have more in-depth discourse. He always felt that McGovern was fulfilling an obligation to Trope & Co., rather than visiting Pavel out of any affection that he might have for him.

"Have you ever been in love?" asked Pavel.

Robert's eyes widened, alarmed.

"You know that is not possible for us. Are you saying you have?" asked Robert with concern. "You have never *acted* upon that desire in any of the houses for that sort of thing, I hope. Please say you have not?"

Pavel shook his head and talked while eating his stew. "No. I am, however, familiar with the female form. Many of the costume fittings are in the workshop and the few actresses who have graced us with their talents have not been shy about changing their costumes in front of the puppet maker."

"My word. How very modern of them," said Robert, clutching both hands to his heart in mock surprise.

"I don't think I stand out very much," Pavel had never given it much thought, but the actors did seem to behave as if he was not in the room.

Robert sat back and studied Pavel. "You are not much to look at," he said.

Pavel smirked. "It has been a blessing that I am not. No one notices the plain puppet maker in the workshop who has never left. On stage, I am nothing more than a voice behind a puppet."

Robert got up from his seat and stretched his arms above his head and walked around the small space that would be his temporary residence. He picked up objects and put them back down, perused a stack of books on a table, touched the fabric on one of the chairs. He eyed the walls where a few paintings hung that Pavel had acquired over time.

"You never travelled? Got the wanderlust to see the

world?"

"No. I read books." Pavel indicated the stack of books Robert had examined.

"I look at the pictures and drawings. I acquire art. I use the library at Mr. Trope's office—he has quite a collection of books. You did say you are familiar with Mr. Trope—did you see him when you arrived here?" Pavel asked.

"Indeed I did," said Robert.

"You were in Trope's offices in America?" Pavel asked.

"Indeed I was. They were most helpful after a rather awful situation I found myself in." Robert's expression grew serious.

So McGovern was telling the truth when he said he and Peters were traveling to New York to work in one of the other offices.

"I had heard they had offices there. I suppose I did not believe they existed."

Robert studied Pavel, again, his expression changing from concern to alarm. "I think perhaps you may have been a bit too sheltered for one of our kind, my dear."

Pavel shrugged. "I study. I have even managed to learn a few words of some of the different languages."

"So, in addition to being rather plain to look at, you are a rather boring fellow as well," said Robert.

"I suppose I am. But I am comfortable," Pavel answered. He changed the subject. "May I ask about your scars?"

"Which ones?"

"I'm sorry. The ones across your back are horrible. Did they happen in your country?"

"If you mean, did they happen in America, yes."

Pavel continued with his questioning. He had never met anyone who was from anywhere so far away. "America is quite different, isn't it?"

"An understatement."

"It wasn't because you are—"

"Oh, heavens no. I am an actor, my dear. I can act the part of the strong and masculine African if I must. No, I have never been persecuted for that, thank goodness. I hear the jail cells for that sort of thing in America are quite uncomfortable. No, I assure you, my scars were acquired during the beginning of the American Civil war. I had the bright idea to go release my indignation upon the ranks of the Confederacy."

"I'm sorry. The Americans did that?"

"Has Trope taught you *nothing*? We are not people who can simply go out and release our anger upon the world when we feel so moved. There are consequences. Punishments." Robert moved to the kitchen hutch where there was another bottle of wine and he opened it, found two glasses and poured for himself and his new friend. Pavel looked at his hands and averted his gaze from Robert. He was frightened and unsure of what to say or ask next.

"People who worked for Mr. Trope… extracted me from my commission in the army and I was brought before a committee. My sentence was one lash for every year I had been alive. And one lash for…" Mr. Lamb did not finish the sentence.

Pavel drained his glass and poured another.

"Don't look so stricken. Not your fault, my dear. I'm sure you would have had the desire to fight for the right side if you had been there. Such injustice. You look a bit on the young side, but they would have taken anyone, I'm sure. But it was wrong. What I did was wrong."

Pavel attempted to make sense of what Robert was telling him. Years of living in the same town, in the same culture, with a limited worldview, despite making weekly trips to the offices of Trope & Co. to collect the mountain of books he had read over time, had never given him any indication of the existence of the world Robert was describing, or any world outside his own, for that matter. Their world. The world of Pavel and Robert and the people who worked for Trope and all the others living in the world who might be like Pavel had consequences and beatings.

Robert continued. "I made my way to Europe as quickly as I could find passage. Showed up on the doorstep of a theatre in France and stayed for a bit before moving on. But you weren't asking about that, *were* you? As for the other scars, the ones on my shoulders... my family died when I was young from the plague or the wasting sickness, or something. My mother died giving birth to me."

"That is exactly what happened with me," said Pavel. "They used to tell me that I killed them all."

Robert challenged Pavel. "Did you?"

"What?"

Robert shook his head. "It angers me, how little you have been educated. I must have a word with Mr. Trope when I go into town. Of course you killed them!"

The color drained from Pavel's face and he stood up, the chair falling over as he did so. He swayed a little on his feet, the alcohol hitting him.

"My dear, I refuse to believe you have been given no instruction on our... abilities. Trope, miserable man that he is, would not be that irresponsible."

Pavel debated on what to say to Robert next. Pavel acknowledged at that moment that his trust of anyone associated with Leonard Trope was quite limited, though his new friend seemed to trust Trope quite completely.

"I did not wish to believe it. There is much that Trope has said to me over the years that I have difficulty with." Pavel continued to sway a bit on his feet but managed to lean over and pick up the chair he had knocked down. He set it down with the deliberate care of one who has had too much to drink and wishes to appear sober. When the chair was returned to its standing position, he again sat. Robert continued talking, though Pavel was experiencing a swirling in his ears, fear and adrenalin coursing through him. Could Mr. Trope have been telling him the truth all this time? He thought Trope made up all the ridiculous rules to scare him and to scare Prochazka and Nina. He had no idea why someone would do that, but he was such a horrible man. Pavel always assumed he was a liar. He thought they were all liars. Why did he decide that? The swirling in his ears let up and he concentrated on what Robert was telling him.

Robert took Pavel's hand and held it with both of his own. "My dear man, we cannot afford to ignore anything Trope says to us. Adopting the idea that he is being disingenuous with you is dangerous, not only to you but to everyone around you."

"I have difficulty imagining that there are that many of us to keep an eye on."

Robert sighed before answering. "I should think there are, though as I said, I do hope not. The world is a big place. It seems that if a handful of us are born in each place that exists, then there are more than quite a few by now."

"Then we *can* have children?"

"*What*? I am about to become quite angry with you, Pavel, for I think you are toying with me, pretending to be ignorant. Or worse, you are in some sort of egregious denial. No. We can't. Of course we can't. I was referring to the accident of *our* birth into the families unlucky enough to receive us."

"What did they tell *you* about the scars and what caused them?" Pavel asked again.

Robert regarded Pavel before answering.

"I believe I should be asking *you* that question, since it appears you have chosen to forget all your lessons. Whoever told you that you are immature appears to be quite correct in that assessment."

Pavel examined the nail beds of his fingers, as if some answer might be found there that was alluding him. His memory problem plagued him again. What had McGovern taught him? What had his parents also taught him? Breathe. The years he had spent alone with only superficial interaction with the various theatre people coming in and out of the theatre and wandering backstage during a show had, despite their presence, exacerbated a certain madness or denial in Pavel born of his extreme loneliness. The idea that he was some sort of angel of death, for want of a better term, was an unacceptable concept, a scientific impossibility. It could not be true. None of it could be true. He avoided the focused stare of his new friend.

"I am an escaped puppet," said Pavel. "Someone cut my strings and I ran away until I made my way home."

The two men sat across the table from each other

without speaking for what seemed to be hours. Pavel finally broke the silence.

"The matter of Mr. Cerny—" Pavel said.

"Oh, heavens. We will go to Mr. Trope in the morning and ask him to find a theatre that plans to do *Hamlet* and have them send a commission for Mr. Cerny. He'll run at the chance and forget all about me, us, the little puppet theatre in Prague, the moment he utters his first *'To be or not to be.'* Don't you agree?" Pavel considered his proposal.

"I need to have a word with Mr. Trope about quite a few things," said Robert. "It will be all right, Pavel. Don't worry. You have a friend in me. You have a friend. It appears you need one. Very much."

"It is hard to have secrets," Pavel said.

Robert shook his head and walked into the bedroom, shutting the door behind him.

After shutting the door to his new living arrangement, and leaving his new friend sitting in the kitchen, Robert put both hands to his face and stifled a sob. He could not speak to him any more tonight. The memories were so recent and still so hideous. They gave the man nightmares. How could his new friend be so ignorant regarding the most dangerous element inherent to their kind? Did Pavel really have no idea what they were designed to do on this Earth?

"Remember Fort Pillow!" He remembered the battle cry that died in his throat as he yelled it. He had been so filled with anger, so filled with rage. A huge roar came out of his throat that seemed to emanate from the very core of his being, then exploded outward. Running, hitting, shooting, stabbing, then more running. His blood burned—his eyes saw red—but it wasn't the blood of his comrades or the Confederate soldiers they had attacked in retaliation. He stopped only when he realized that he was the only person standing. His eyes cleared of their rage and he saw it. A spiral of death that started at his feet and spread in a circular fashion away from him like a great, round tapestry woven of bodies spread as far as the eye could see, bathed in their own blood. Blood had gushed from noses, ears, and eyes. So much blood—a deep red mixed with an even greater amount of fluid that was more violet in color, then a clear liquid, like water—continued to run from every orifice. White soldiers so pale, their veins stood out in blue relief against translucent skin. Black soldiers a sickening pale, gray, chalky color, the whites of their open eyes a horrific shade of pale blue. Everyone was dead or dying. Not only the enemy they were there to challenge, but Robert's fellows. Everyone. Robert stood alone, terrified. He fell to his knees and retched until he thought his ribs would break. Eighteen years ago. That eighteen years amounted to what seemed no more than a minute in Robert's lifetime.

Robert had been in Tennessee. The Civil War raged, and Robert became inflamed with anger upon learning of one senseless, bloody, and brutal incident. Fort Pillow. April 12, 1864. Robert felt a primal need to do something. Confederate Major General Nathan Bedford Forrest had attacked the fort with a cavalry division of approximately 2,500 men. Out of 262 colored troops in the Union garrison at Fort Pillow, only 62 survived. The massacre was believed to be a deliberate slaughter of colored troops. Robert joined one of a few units of black soldiers retaliating against

Confederates for the massacre. The adopted avenging battle cry was, "Remember Fort Pillow!"

Robert had been warned, schooled about who and what he was and the importance of his emotions being kept under control, that his passions could not be allowed to best him. His sense of injustice in this instance overwhelmed him to the point that his dominant nature took hold and he became that thing that people like Mr. Trope worked so hard to ensure against. Robert Lamb became an angel of death that day.

Later, he was brought before a committee of his peers, who chose to spare his life and spread a vague story of him surviving the battle and deserting that day. Robert was relocated immediately to Europe. The lashes on his back were a reminder. One for every year of his life and one for each person who died on the battlefield that day. Robert would never again doubt the power available to him if he ever went out of control again.

Pavel listened to the muffled sobs coming from behind the door of Robert's room. He did not move from the table. He sat, wide-eyed, all night, and only got up to retreat to his cot in the workshop as the sun began to rise.

Chapter 14

Kevin: Present Day

Kevin wandered through the bike shop and glanced at various objects without focusing on any of them with any degree of interest. He was busy watching the boy in the black t-shirt with the anarchy symbol—a white circle with an exaggerated upper case A in the middle. The boy wore a wool beanie over dyed black hair, black skinny jeans slung low over his hips, black high-top athletic shoes and a backpack to finish off the look. He matched the appearance of a thousand other boys in the area. Kevin marveled at the way his peers claimed to dress to express their individuality, and yet they managed to look like everyone else with the same idea. What they wanted was to conform, to fit in, to blend in so as not to be noticed. Getting noticed might result in someone stronger beating the shit out of them. The thinking went something like that, Kevin knew. Kevin had dressed the part before coming to the shop, and was wearing almost identical clothing except Kevin's t-shirt was plain black. He had an extra change of identical clothing in his own backpack. The uniform reminded Kevin of the house he had visited and the family inside. Everything identical. Everything conforming. Kevin found something offensive about anything that celebrated such ordinary sameness. The uniform was close enough that if anyone asked later, no one would be able to distinguish which boy was which and who followed whom. Did they arrive or leave together? No one would know or remember because "all those kids look alike to me." Kevin had heard it a thousand times.

"I told you, it's over here!" said Kevin. He turned to the teenage boy who'd followed him from the bike shop on Saticoy to Reseda Boulevard, deep in the San Fernando Valley. The bike shop had wheel replacements for Kevin's skateboard, and though plenty of other shops closer to Kevin's home had what he needed, Kevin wanted to have a little fun and preferred to venture out of the neighborhood. Kevin put his skateboard on the ground, pulled on a pair of gloves that had built-in wrist guards, hopped on the skateboard and rode down the street. The gullible boy followed him on his bike, lured by the promise of a bag of pot.

"I stole it from my uncle," Kevin told the boy. "It's medical, so it's really strong. He's got PTSD or some shit like that, so that's why he has it. Anyway, I got some and stashed it under the bridge on Reseda Boulevard." They were near the bridge overlooking the Los Angeles River, a meandering concrete channel that started in the San Fernando Valley and ran for about forty-eight miles through various parts of the Los Angeles basin. Often empty or near empty, the channel served as a camp for homeless people who set up shelters under the various bridges and overpasses that ran the length of the river. The riverbed was also a good place to hide things.

Kevin hopped off his skateboard, vaulted over the concrete railing and onto the ground on the other side. He worked his way down the embankment to an area far underneath the bridge. "C'mon!" he called to the kid. What had he said his name was? Josh? Ian? Some generic name for a generic boy. The boy got off his bike.

"What about my bike?" the boy called.

"Shit, you're right." Did he have to make it so easy? Kevin went back up to the concrete railing. "Here, hand it over the railing to me. We'll hide it here." The boy hoisted the bike over the railing to Kevin, who leaned it against the concrete on the other side, making it invisible from the boulevard.

They moved together down the embankment and under the bridge. Kevin did another quick look around to see if the area was occupied. All clear. No blankets, lean-to tents or large boxes that might serve to hide someone choosing to camp in that location. Kevin led the way to the seam between bridge and channel at the topmost part of the embankment. Dirt and weeds came through the concrete where part of the channel had broken up over time.

"Right here. Kevin started digging around in an area of dirt. The boy kneeled next to him. "Can you hand me that hunk of concrete right there? No, the bigger one." The boy handed Kevin a hunk of concrete. He did not even ask Kevin what he meant to do with it. Kevin took the hunk of concrete and smashed it full into the boy's face. After the boy fell to the ground, Kevin continued to smash the boy's face and head until the boy would never move again. Kevin stripped off his clothes until he stood naked under the bridge and proceeded to turn his soiled clothes inside out, using the inside of the shirt and jeans to wipe off his face, arms and hair. He took the extra change of clothing out of his backpack and put them on. When he was cleaned off and dressed, Kevin sauntered back to the concrete railing. He glanced once at the bike as he picked up his skateboard, hopped back over the railing and took off down the street where he would catch the bus back to his own part of town. Behind him lay the remains of the generic teenage boy who would be found eventually, though it was probable the first discovery would be made by coyotes. Kevin skated for a few blocks and deposited his backpack with the bloody clothing into a trash bin near a bus stop. He kept the other backpack that had belonged to the boy. No one would look in the trash. Kevin knew this area. He knew that bus stop. People threw the most disgusting things in that trash bin. Baggies of dog poop, diapers changed at the bus stop, human filth of every variety. Confident, Kevin remained at that very bus stop waiting for the arrival of the next bus.

Kevin had left his digital recorder at home, so no music would accompany this killing, but there is always merit in variety, thought Kevin.

Chapter 15

1883

"Father, I have decided I wish to marry Pavel and move to America."

Pavel and Eduard Rychtar stared, open-mouthed, at Žophie, both men surprised and stunned. They sat at the dining table in the Rychtar home and had enjoyed a quiet evening meal when Žophie made her announcement. Rychtar's eyes flashed.

"Sir, I assure you I am as surprised by her as you are. Žophie, what mischief are you up to now?" Pavel asked.

"None. I think it is time you and I were married, and I want to move to America."

"Žophie, this is highly inappropriate. You do know it is customary for the man to ask the woman for her hand.

And that comes after the man has had the opportunity to discuss things with the woman's father. That's me, in case you have forgotten."

"I don't care. If I wait to be asked, I'll be a toothless old crone. Pavel, you weren't going to ask me unless I asked you. Were you?"

Pavel was silent.

"And Táta, it was not as if you were approaching Pavel to see what his intentions were or when he planned on making those intentions known. You are both slow as turtles."

"I fail to see what the rush is. We have been spending a good amount of time getting to know one another," Rychtar said.

"Yes, and you and Pavel already have business that you conduct with one another. I know this." Žophie was referring to a parcel of land that the two had invested in together and were in discussion with several architects regarding building plans. The past year had proved to be a positive year for Pavel and Eduard Rychtar as friends first, then colleagues.

"Does Pavel have any say in this matter of yours, daughter? You are rather putting him in a corner, aren't you? And at dinner?"

"Pavel? Tell me you don't want to marry me and go to America."

"Mr. Rychtar, it appears that things have gotten away from us somehow, and I have no choice in the matter but to try to attach some normalcy to the proceedings. I know this is irregular, and no, this has not been discussed prior to this moment, but if you would do me the honor of granting me your daughter's hand, I would be most grateful."

"No! You don't get to take this away from me," said Žophie. "This is my proposal. My idea. Either you want to or not, but you don't get to try to twist it around to being normal and boring and predictable. Father? I would like to marry Pavel and move to America. Apparently he wants to marry me. So?"

"Žophie, why America? They just had a war—" Eduard said.

"That was almost twenty years ago, and I don't want to go to that part," she said. Žophie got up from the table and ran out of the room. The two men exchanged a look, shook their heads and laughed. Pavel felt a host of emotions and was trying not to breathe for fear of blurting out—what, he wasn't sure. A laugh, a cry, a wail of despair. Žophie reentered the room carrying a pile of papers and pamphlets and books.

"The location is in a place called California—nowhere near where they had the war. The weather is beautiful all the time, and people are moving there from all the colder places in the country to be there. They are building such grand and unusual homes—look!"

"How on earth did you come by these pamphlets? What would you possibly know about America?" asked Eduard.

"Father, you did not raise me to be an idiot. Pavel is a self-educated man. Why can't I follow his example and educate myself about things in the world other than our tiny little existence here? I want to go where it is new. It is in an area in the San Gabriel Valley near the mountains along a river they call the Arroyo Seco. Look at these illustrations! It is beautiful. They are calling it the Indiana Colony of California."

The men examined the pile of paper collected by Žophie and then at each other.

"And I wish to marry Pavel and go there."

"Pavel? Do you wish to have any say in the matter? Do you have any desire to leave your work, your theatre?" asked Eduard.

Pavel spoke with care. He was attempting to control his breathing and reduce his rapid heartbeat, but it was taking some effort. "Žophie, I would very much like to be your husband. But America?" He could not believe his fortune. This beautiful woman loved *him*.

"All right! Fine, you two go talk about it or talk to your people or go look around your theatre and ask your puppets or do whatever it is that you do, but I expect an answer."

"Žophie, I don't know what to do with you," said her father.

Pavel stood. "This evening has become very odd and has given me much to think about. If you don't mind, I will excuse myself for the evening. I believe I have been assigned the task of making a decision. Žophie. Eduard. I will speak with you both on another day."

Žophie ran to him. "You are not upset? Tell me you are not upset, Pavel. You do want to marry me, yes?"

Dear Mr. Trusnik:

It is of the utmost urgency that we see you at our offices at Trope & Co. A matter has come to our attention that requires our immediate action. It is of the utmost urgency that we speak with you regarding your association with one Žophie Rychtar, daughter of Judge Eduard Rychtar. The matter, while urgent, is of a delicate nature and will be handled with all appropriate discretion.

Sincerely,
Leonard Trope

Mr. Trope told Pavel that in his present state of denial he was becoming a danger to himself and to others. The letters stated that Pavel had no idea how dangerous he actually was. He had a drawer full of warning letters, all outlining why it was imperative that he cease his association with Žophie Rychtar, and he had read all of these letters and summarily dismissed them. Did they not tell him he could *hope?* Pavel meant to marry Žophie.

"Žophie, you must allow me some time to think, yes?" Pavel stumbled out the door, and halfway between the Rychtar home and his workshop lodgings he collapsed on the side of the road. Anxiety had caused a stitch in his side that was making it difficult for Pavel to walk or breathe. He doubled over and threw up at the side of the road. America? Married? He had never left here. His family was here. Well, the theatre was here, which was a monument to his family. How could he leave that? She was asking him for the impossible. Yet a part of him wanted, for her, to make it possible.

Pavel thought of a million ways to break his association with her. He had begun the conversation countless times in his head, how he was not meant to be with anyone, how she had greater prospects than he, how he had no plans to travel the globe. His rehearsed speeches fell flat. He had no resolve when it came to Žophie, for he had fallen hopelessly in love. Pavel meant to marry Žophie, and he hoped with every fiber of his being that Mr. Trope and all the worrying souls who sent him letters of warning, were simply that. Worrying souls. Nothing bad could come of this. This was love. There was nothing greater and more hopeful than love.

"Behold. Unloved vegetables," Žophie said. Only yesterday had Žophie announced that she intended to marry Pavel, and he was still wrestling with the host of emotions at war with his reason. They sat under a tree surrounded by boulders which provided a makeshift table and chairs for an outdoor luncheon. Žophie had brought a stew of lamb and potato, with the addition of several root vegetables which Pavel quite liked: rutabaga, turnip, parsnip, carrot and beet. Pavel stared at them, overjoyed.

"You cooked them yourself!" he said.

"With a great degree of reluctance!" Žophie countered.

"I happen to love all root vegetables. It does them a great injustice to call them 'unloved,'" he said, smiling.

"I would call it an injustice to make us eat them!" she said, returning his smile. Pavel loved her smile. And her laugh made every place *sound* better, by changing whatever outside noise his ear might register to something musical and happy.

One year ago, Žophie had walked through the door of his workshop. She made him happy. Hopeful.

He ate his turnips and rutabagas and parsnips and was content with the beautiful day. One thing marred the otherwise perfect afternoon, and that was the fifth letter of warning from Trope & Co. regarding his association with Žophie which resided as a crumpled ball in the pocket of Pavel's trousers. He knew, without reading, what they wished to speak with him about, and it did not involve making the room a better place or laughter or happiness. Or hope.

"What is making you look so serious, Pavel?" asked Žophie.

"Do I look serious? How rude of me. That was not my intention. I was thinking about a new design for one of my puppets, but it involves a very special element."

"What kind of element?"

"Your face."

"What? My face?"

Pavel decided if there was a possibility he would never see her again, there was one thing he could do to keep a bit of her with him.

"I would like to make a puppet in the likeness of the most beautiful woman I know."

"Oh, Pavel! How wonderful! What can I do? Wait. Did you say the *most beautiful* woman you know?"

"I suppose I did. I might have been lying. You can never be sure when people are talking about puppets. They all lie."

Žophie pushed him into the clover that grew at the base of the boulders. He rolled and landed upon his knees. He laughed and stood, and noticed the green clover stain on his knee. He laughed and shrugged.

"It will require a certain amount of patience on your

part. And no squirming whatsoever, or the results will be quite awful," said Pavel.

"Sounds so mysterious!" she said.

"Not so much. I take a plaster cast of your face, leaving you room to breathe, of *course*, and once the plaster dries, I have a perfect outline of your face."

Žophie studied him for a moment, looking a little unsure. If she had misgivings, she dismissed them, for she threw her hands in the air and laughed.

"You are so very creative!"

"Oh, I am not the first to try this, I can assure you. Would you want to? I'm afraid it will leave a small bit of a mess, but you can wash up with little or no evidence of our silliness."

"Can we do it right now?" Žophie asked and put away the lunch plates and utensils.

"But I haven't finished my 'unloved vegetables,'" Pavel said.

"They'll have to wait. This is too exciting!"

With that, the couple walked back to the workshop. Pavel tried not to think about the letter from Trope that was crumpled in his pocket.

Robert Lamb entered the workshop, hearing laughter from his friend. Pavel stood over the workbench, his hands in heavy gloves which were covered with some sort of gooey white substance. Below him, a woman with a large glob of plaster completely covering her face leaned back in a chair, and straws protruded from her nose and mouth. She appeared to be shaking with laughter.

Robert approached, keeping his face neutral. He had been watching Pavel's friendship grow with Žophie. He had been spoken to by Mr. Trope and was quite concerned.

"No, you can't move, you'll crack it!" Pavel said. He noticed Robert and waved him into the room. "Okay, Robert has entered the room. Don't be startled when he starts to talk. I don't want you to go and do something silly like jump up and start running around the room, screaming."

"Will he, nill he?" Robert quoted *Hamlet*.

"Cheidu, you are uncannily on time. How would you like to have yourself immortalized?" The two men shared a look. Robert raised his eyebrow at his friend and smirked.

"You mean keep this young and handsome face *forever*?" he said. Pavel punched him in the arm.

"I need to make a plaster cast of your face. To make your puppet!"

"Ah! A doppelganger! How thrilling. Pavel, you are a constant source of amazement to me. Where would you like me to drape myself?" Pavel led his friend over to a chair and positioned him.

"Are you comfortable?" asked Pavel.

"Oh, without question. Out of curiosity, how long will this remain on my face? I have a tea engagement later."

"Not too long. I don't want you to start itching."

Before long, Pavel had both Žophie and Robert leaning back in their respective chairs in the workshop, plaster over their faces, straws out of their noses and mouths, both able only to groan in protest at anything Pavel had to say.

"I believe this is the one and only time I will find either one of you absolutely speechless," Pavel said. "In fact, I believe this is the one and only time I will ever find myself in complete control of anything that has anything to do with anything where either one of you are concerned."

His friends groaned.

"Oh, I assure you, when this is all over, you'll thank me. I plan on making beautiful carvings of you both. Young and beautiful forever, my escaped puppets, yes?"

Žophie's groan was lilting and sounded more like a question.

"Ah yes, Žophie, you aren't familiar with the story my ancestor used to tell about his family members. He called them all his escaped puppets. I am but a mere descendant of a long line of them, leading back to Prochazka, founder of the theatre."

After the plaster was dry on both of them, Pavel removed it, first from Žophie and then from Robert. He turned the masks to show the inside that had been against their faces and watched their reactions as they saw the contours of their own faces.

"Fascinating," said Robert.

"That is a little unnerving," said Žophie. "It is almost like a death mask."

"Oh don't say that! It will be beautiful. You have to trust me," said Pavel.

"Thank you, Pavel," said Robert. "I look forward to seeing my double. We can do all the plays where twins are featured. *Comedy of Errors*, anyone? Can we put white face on a puppet?"

Pavel laughed and gave Robert another playful punch in the arm. "I love you all, madly, but must dash off to tea! I expect those puppets to be gorgeous!" Robert swept out of the theatre as Pavel and Žophie laughed.

When Robert returned to the workshop, several hours later, he found Pavel still busy at the workbench, creating a template for the wood carving he would do of the face masks. He created their faces out of clay as a first step in the process, molding and sculpting and making a three dimensional image which would serve as a template when later making his wood carving.

"My good man, you do work late," said Robert.

"It is not very late. Is it? Have you come from dinner? Would you like to have something to eat?"

"I was supposed to have tea, but I'm afraid there was more whiskey than tea and very little food, so yes. Yes, I'm starved. Back to the house?"

"Yes. Tell me. What do you think of you?" Pavel held up the clay bust of Robert that he had been working on. Robert walked over, a little unsteady after his tea that was more whiskey. He scrutinized the bust, turning the base so that he could review all sides of the creation.

"You are a very gifted artist, Pavel. It looks wonderful. But I do have magnificent bone structure for this sort of thing to make it easy for you. Thank you. It is quite moving to have an artist capture one's image in a form like that."

"You're welcome. In finished form, it will be a marionette. About your size, I think. Rod and wire."

"Even more impressive. Be sure to make me a good-looking puppet. Some of them can be so hideous and frightening."

"That is because they are supposed to be," said Pavel.

"Can't have crones or devils or dwarfs or monsters that are painted in pastels and have pretty smiles on their faces."

"No, I think not. Shall we to dinner?"

The two men walked to Robert Lamb's house and worked together to create a dinner. They were silent while each did their part, but the two did not need conversation. Since Robert's brief residency, the men had grown to be quite close, and a brotherly bond existed between them. Not until the dinner was set upon the table, the wine poured and the two men seated did conversation begin.

"Žophie has informed both me and her father that she means for us to marry and move to America," said Pavel. He was nervous and concentrated on his breathing. He searched his friend's face for his reaction to the news.

Robert choked a bit on his wine. "Are you serious?"

"Yes."

"Married? America?"

"Yes. Some place in the south of California in a settlement called the Indiana Colony. She already has the plans for the house she wants there."

"You. Marrying Žophie." Robert put down his fork and sat back.

"She is very persuasive when she wants something. I believe she will have that house."

Robert took a sip of his wine and weighed his words. "Have you received any correspondence from Mr. Trope about this?"

Pavel did not mention the numerous letters of warning. Trope did not know about the plans to marry, so it was not a complete lie.

"Trope doesn't know."

"I see," said Robert.

Pavel saw the horror on his friend's face. "What's wrong?"

"Pavel you know you cannot marry. *We* cannot marry. How many times must it be repeated to you? Our kind cannot marry. It is not done. You know the consequences, or do you not care?" A lone tear meandered down Robert's cheek. Pavel stared at him.

"Cheidu, what's wrong?"

"Let me ask you a question. The whipping scars on my back. Do they not serve as an example to you? We cannot run off and do whatever we want when other people are involved."

Robert shook his head, stood up and paced around the room, disgusted.

"Your parents. Prochazka and Nina. Were they affectionate with you?"

"Of course they were. They were very affectionate people."

"How did they express it? Did they hug you? Kiss your forehead? Pinch your cheeks? Smother you in kisses when you were a good boy?"

"No, nothing like that, we had a thing we did as a family. As a puppet family. We played a game Prochazka made up when I was very small."

"Did it involve touching you in any way?"

Pavel remembered the day in Trope's office when he realized that they had avoided touching their son his entire life. He did not share the memory with his friend.

"No, but I didn't like to be touched when I was a boy."

"So they told you this was for you? Because you did not like to be touched?"

"Well, I outgrew that. But the game kept on."

"Because they could not touch you."

"Perhaps this dinner needs to be over."

"Pavel, you cannot marry that girl!"

"You're jealous. That's what it is."

Robert looked like a man who had been slapped. He rose from the table, his chair scraping on the floor behind him.

"Don't be ridiculous. And do not flatter yourself. If you decided you wanted to up and move to America, yes. I would miss you. We have barely met in terms of our years. And America is not a good place for me to visit, so it would be many years before we could see each other again. So, yes, I would miss you very much. But this is not about that. This is about people like us. We cannot get close to others. We cannot touch, we cannot hold, we cannot kiss, we cannot *love.*"

"I refuse to believe that. Your scars happened as a punishment for acting out of anger. Not out of love. We know that from every great playwright and play: Shakespeare, the Greek plays, Faust, and Moliere. When there is anger or jealousy or rage or plotting or greed, then nothing good comes at the end of any of those stories. But when people act out of love, nothing bad can happen and everyone is blessed. I am in love. *Nothing* bad can come from love. I won't believe it. Love gives everyone hope, and isn't that what we are supposed to do? Bring hope, not destruction? What is more hopeful than love?"

"Pavel, this is not a play, though you are playing a very

dangerous game. I refuse to believe you intend to go through with this. Are you that selfish, or completely insane? Which is it? Be Žophie's friend. Be her confidante, be that wonderful man that makes her laugh with his puppetry. But Pavel, please. Do not try to be her lover. For her sake."

"I don't wish to talk to you any more about this. I mean to leave you in charge of the artistic aspects of the theatre and will have Mr. Trope take care of having the property transferred to you upon my leaving for America. I do not wish to be interfered with beyond that."

"Pavel, please do not do this thing."

"You cannot tell me that I cannot love. How can you tell someone that they are not allowed to love? You? You of all people." Pavel got up from the table and left the house.

Robert sat at the table and wept.

Chapter 16

1884

Pavel and Žophie landed in a heap on the floor of the foyer, Žophie laughing as Pavel slammed the door behind them with his foot. Her laughing was smothered by his mouth, kissing, searching, tongues meeting, tasting, exploring. His fingers shook as they struggled with the fasteners on the back of her dress. Her hands, inexperienced and eager, tugged at his shirt, pulling it out of the waist of his pants, running over his bare torso underneath and around to his back. Pavel moved his mouth to her neck, over her collarbone and chest, moving closer to her breasts as he continued to work his way through her dress fastenings. Žophie laughed again and Pavel joined her, the two of them tangled together upon the floor in an unceremonious heap.

Months of travel in separate berths, bunks and cabins that kept them apart made their longing for one another an ever growing and intense ache that was finally seeing relief now that the two could finally come together as husband and wife.

"We stink," said Žophie.

"Isn't it wonderful," said Pavel, his mouth over hers again as he kissed her. His hand moved down and pulled up the fabric on her dress. He moved his hand up her leg and over her thigh. He stopped kissing her and looked in her eyes as his hand made contact with the moist area between her legs. Žophie placed her hand on his to keep it there as she matched his gaze. She guided his hand over her, rubbing, caressing. He pulled down her undergarments until his naked hand was upon her, unimpeded by fabric. He moved his mouth down her body, over her breasts still bound by her dress and corset, down her bodice, then pushed her dress up and over her hips and put his mouth full upon her sex, inhaling her, kissing her. Žophie cried out, and he tasted her, caressed her with his tongue. While their longing for each other had raged for months the two remained chaste, but the longing Pavel experienced in the foyer encompassed one hundred fifty years and involved more than the final consummation of the marriage to this woman he adored. Rather, what he was experiencing was the letting go of a lifetime of forced loneliness and avoidance of other people. He felt as if he had been freed from a prison. Consumed by passion, Pavel felt as if his entire person might burst into flame at that very moment and if it did, he would not care. Žophie worked her hands over his trousers until she got them almost off of him, enough that they could find each other. He entered her, and she cried out again as the two of them moved together as one, newlyweds who had travelled a very long way by ship, by cart, then on foot, filthy and stinking, in a pile of partially removed clothing, the hard floor beneath them bruising them as they rolled and moved as one for the first time.

He rolled onto his side and laughed, tracing her face with his finger. "I had no idea," said Žophie who joined his laughter.
"Nor did I," Pavel said.
"You have never?"
"Never. Only you."
"Well, Pavel Trusnik."
"Yes, Žophie Trusnik?"
"I think we should do this some more, don't you?"
Pavel laughed again. How Žophie made him laugh.
"Shall we have a bath, first?"
"Is there a bath?"
"Every modern convenience for my bride. No expense spared. I did, after all, promise your father."
Later in the bath, finally naked, they bathed each other, each staring at the other as they explored and touched and admired each other's bodies.
"I think the corset is a horrible invention," said Pavel.
"You are not alone in that thought," she said, and seemed pensive. "You never went to those houses in town—"
"Never."
"I don't believe you. How do you know what to do, to do that—"
"I do not spend all my time carving the faces of

marionettes or putting on puppet theatre, you know. I have read a book or two."

"There are books about—"

"Everything. Why do you think this theatre rat is so good at drawing up plumbing design plans for the construction of your new bath? What do you think of your bath, by the way?"

"It is beautiful. I plan on spending my entire life in here."

"I hope not!" He pulled her to him and kissed her again.

"What day were you born?" she asked.

"What?"

"What day of the week were you born?"

"Wednesday, I think. I don't know."

"*Wednesday's child is full of woe.* Are you?"

"I have no idea what you're talking about," said Pavel.

"The poem! *Monday's child is fair of face, Tuesday's child is full of grace, Wednesday's child is full of woe, Thursday's child has far to go, Friday's child is loving and giving, Saturday's child works hard for a living, But the child who is born on the Sabbath Day is bonny and blithe and good and gay.*"

"So if you're born on Church Sunday, all is well?"

Žophie snuggled into him. "It's a poem. But you do sometimes appear sad to me. Are you sad now?"

"I think sad and woe might be different, but no, I am not sad now. I am the happiest I have ever been in my entire life. And that is saying something." He laughed.

They made love again, facing each other in the tub, the water splashing over them. Pavel had never been so happy. He looked into her eyes.

"I love you."
At that moment, Žophie's nose started to bleed.

Chapter 17

Kevin: Present Day

Kevin examined the contents of a cigar box he'd found when looking through the backpack he'd stolen from the generic boy from the bike shop. The backpack would serve as a souvenir of his day, slumming in Reseda. He did not go there very often. A blighted area. Very neglected. Graffiti sprayed not only on fences and walls, but on trees. What kind of person tags a tree? It had been raining when he left Reseda, and when he returned to Pasadena, the sun was shining and there was no sign of a storm.

He studied the cigar box, which was old and more than likely, had belonged to someone else before the generic boy got ahold of it, a grandparent, perhaps. He lifted the lid and found a rolled up length of red embroidery thread, and an expired passport. Generic boy must have gone somewhere with his family? He turned the pages to look for stamps. Guatemala, Peru, Mexico. Guess the family had a thing for South America. He read the name. Josh Aloyan. Armenian. He found a stack of post-it notes with words scrawled on them. They appeared to be random quotes from children's stories by authors such as Lemony Snicket and Hans Christian Andersen, for the authors were credited next to the quotes on the post-it. They meant nothing to him.

"Honestly," Kevin said aloud. "Why do people save this shit?"

Kevin used his sleeve to wipe down the cigar box and tossed it into the garbage can near the cafe by the bus stop. Enough food would be thrown away in the garbage can that the cigar box, and its contents, could be destroyed within a day. He had second thoughts about keeping the backpack and went around to the dumpster located in the parking lot behind the cafe. He wiped down the pack with his sleeve while wearing his skater gloves, then tossed it in the dumpster, along with the gloves.

He skated home and ascended the stairs. He took a moment to look at the Victorian across the street. No flutter of drapes. As usual.

"You're just in time for dinner!" called his mother.

"Great! What are we having?" he responded, ever the dutiful and perfect son.

"Turkey meatloaf."

"'Meatloaf, smeatloaf, double-beatloaf. I hate meatloaf,'" Kevin quoted from *A Christmas Story* as he walked into the spacious kitchen. Unlike the perfectly preserved Victorian across the street, Kevin's parents had done a remodel on their kitchen that included the requisite Sub-Zero refrigerator drawers, glass-fronted cabinets, and granite countertops, the latest suburban remodel trends.

Kevin's mom, a young-looking woman in her mid-forties, playfully swatted him with the spatula. "You love meatloaf," she said.

"I know. I just like saying that. It's funny," he said. "Dad home yet?"

"He has to work late. It's just us. Can you handle it?" His mother set down the plates, added a large bowl of salad to the center of the table and poured herself a glass of Pinot Noir.

"Can I have a glass?"

"Don't push it. Get yourself some water." Kevin poured himself a glass from the filter in the door of the refrigerator.

"How was soccer practice?" his mother asked.

"Oh. You know. Same old." Kevin had not played soccer in months, but his parents had no idea. Their schedules did not allow them to attend games, so Kevin's entire extracurricular schedule was free to do as he pleased during those times they thought he was at practice or at a game. No one at the school had reason to contact them regarding his withdrawal from the team.

"I so totally nailed one guy in the face," Kevin said.

"Kevin! Is he all right?"

"You mean, will he live?" Kevin burst out laughing and didn't answer the question. He stuffed meatloaf in his mouth and watched his mother drink her wine. On the nights his father worked late, he could count on her finishing the bottle and going to bed early.

It was turning out to be a perfect and wonderful day. "Hey, Mom, so, have you ever met the old guy across the street?"

"Mr. Trusnik?" his mother said.

"You *have* met him? You know his *name*? I never knew that."

"I know his name, not him. I can't remember who told me. One of the neighbors. He's been here longer than anyone on the street, though how long that is, I don't know. He inherited the house from his family, according to neighborhood talk. He has family members who are supposedly the original owners. They go back several generations to when Pasadena was not even Pasadena yet."

"They said something about that at school. Iowa Colony, Indiana, something like that?"

"Something like that—that's all you got? Listen harder."

"Whatevs."

Kevin chewed his meatloaf. He looked expectantly at his mother for more information.

"In answer to your question, no, I've never met him. I hear he's a shut-in since his wife died."

"Oh. When did she die?"

"Not sure. Before our time here."

That confirmed to Kevin that there was only one person in the house.

"So nobody has ever seen him? How can that be?"

His mother became impatient. "Why all the questions about an old man? I thought your generation didn't care about old people."

"Our generation. What is that?"

"I don't know. Why do you want to know about him?"

Kevin answered, nonchalant. "Well, he's our neighbor, isn't he? I mean is he okay over there by himself? Does he need anything?"

"I'm sure his family or someone takes care of him."

"Have you ever seen anyone go over there?"

"Kevin, I really haven't given it much attention. I don't spend my time staring at the neighbors' houses. Nor should you. It's rude."

"Whatevs."

"'Whatevs?' What is that? You can't finish words already dismissive enough? You're dismissing the dismissive word. Boggles the mind. What*ever*, yourself. Eat your dinner."

Kevin considered the new information supplied by his mother. *Mr. Trusnik*. He had a name. Kevin could use that when he let himself in.

"Speaking of the neighbors," said Kevin's mother, "did you hear the Hague's cat got killed by a coyote last week? And the Nelsens lost their dachshund as well. Terrible."

"Good thing we don't have a pet," said Kevin.

His mother poured another glass of wine. "It's terrible. You never know. I hear they travel in packs. One will approach and then the others come from out of nowhere and surround the animal before they tear it apart. I heard that a man was walking his dog in Hollywood and was approached by a coyote and then another came out from under a parked car right there on the street. They tore his dog right off the leash in front of him."

"That's kinda cool," said Kevin.

"Okay, no it's not."

Kevin thought about Sprinkles, the Hague's cat, that had been so stupid and trusting when it came up to him and rubbed against his leg. He had snapped Sprinkle's neck without thinking about it. He took it behind his house and started on the carcass with his scalpel, then used the butcher scissors from his mother's knife block to do the rest of the job. He wanted to make it look like a coyote had been lurking in the neighborhood. He kept the eviscerated and decaying body in a plastic bag behind the gardening shed for a couple days before going out at night and dumping it in the Hague's yard—a little something horrible for the kids to see when they left for school the next day. Kevin used to play soccer with the youngest Hague boy, Lance. Kevin didn't like Lance.

As far as the Nelsen's dog, Fred, that was not Kevin, but probably a coyote. Coyotes got credit for a lot of things Kevin did, but they did do a fair amount of damage on their own. Kevin smiled at the thought.

"What are you smiling about?" asked his mother.

"Nothing. I was thinking about something. What's for dessert?"

"Nothing. Eat a banana or something. There might be some cookies in a drawer. Go help yourself." Kevin's mom was starting to get a bit snarky, something she did after a few glasses of wine. It was time for Kevin to make his exit. He would wait after darkness had descended for a few hours before crossing the street.

Chapter 18

1884

Žofie lay in the hospital bed, her wasted body pale and thin, blood drying in the cracks of her lips which could no longer be kissed without causing excruciating pain. Pavel, a young man appearing to be all of eighteen, stood in the waiting area, watching her ravaged form through the filter offered by the distance of the waiting room to her hospital bed. He could see her hospital bed and her wasting body through a sliver of an opening in the doorway. Everything was off. The interior walls were an industrial off-white, the octagonal tile also off-white and scarred with scratches and gouges. The lights flickered from overhead oil lamps giving everything a mottled and distorted appearance, and the air was thick with the smell of human frailty in all its forms:

blood, urine, sweat, vomit, disappointment, impatience, and grief. None of this should be happening. Pavel stood, powerless. He focused on a section of Žofie's arm to shut out the smells and the despair, the anguish masked by alcohol baths and powdered cleansers.

A voice spoke from behind Pavel's shoulder.

"It isn't easy, is it, knowing you're responsible?"

Pavel spun around to see a man standing behind him in the corridor. The man was large, with red hair. He seemed familiar to Pavel, but in his grief he could not place where he might have met him or where he had seen him before. The red-haired man held a hat in one hand and had an overcoat draped over his other arm, which was unusual for the warm weather of Pasadena. Pavel could not discern his age, maybe thirty, maybe fifty. Pavel had never been good with that sort of thing. The stranger held the countenance that Pavel had seen on countless hospital clergy since his and Žophie's arrival, a combination of knowing resignation and hope that only a person in the profession of religion could effectively get away with without appearing to be ridiculous. This particular man, however, had something very different about him. It was his eyes. Where the pupils should be, with their unrevealing darkness surrounded by iris, instead appeared a flickering glow, bluish at first and then amber, then red, then back to blue again and ever changing. Pavel started, for he knew those eyes. The constant changing color and intensity emanating from their center, generating out into the irises, gave them an unnatural depth and knowing quality that frightened Pavel. Yet he thought the eyes seemed familiar—Trope?

"What did you say?" Pavel asked.

"It is never easy. Watching them fade."

Pavel's voice faltered. "Are you the other doctor they sent for? Please tell me what is wrong."

The man's eyes met Pavel's. "You do know what has brought you here?"

Pavel looked back through the sliver of open doorway at Žofie. "They say she has the consumption."

The man grabbed Pavel by the arm and forced him to look him in the eye.

"Pavel. It's McGovern. You know me. It has been years, but you know me."

Pavel started crying.

"McGovern? Yes. I remember you."

McGovern seemed to be very angry, as if he was trying to refrain from striking Pavel in the hospital corridor.

"What will happen to her?" Pavel asked.

McGovern led Pavel to a bench against the wall and sat him down. The large man was breathing long deep breaths in an apparent effort to calm himself.

"You were warned. You were told. You were schooled in your youth. You chose to ignore the advice of people who have been keeping our very existence quiet for hundreds of years. You ignored the experience of your best friend. Did you honestly think you could get away with trying to be normal and no one would get hurt?"

Pavel's gaze held no comprehension.

McGovern continued, speaking in a low voice so as not to be overheard. "Do *not* try to play the ignorant, injured person here. And do not try to act like an old drug user, because that habit ended over a hundred years ago, and you can't claim to suddenly forget who you are. You *know* what this is. You were told under no uncertain terms. Pavel. The Great Rule must not be broken."

McGovern leaned over and put his face in his hands, dejected. Pavel got up and returned to the spot in the corridor outside Žophie's room where he was keeping vigil.

McGovern stayed on the bench, shook his head and crushed his hat between his large hands, helpless.

Žofie died, mere hours later. Pavel's anguished cry, when Žofie's last breath abandoned her, filled the hospital corridor and the one beyond that. He wanted to die as well, but McGovern remained by his side, unrelenting in his reminders and explanations of all that Pavel knew already, but chose to deny the moment he and Žofie stepped on the gangplank to the ship that brought them to America. Pavel's death would not come for quite some time. Žofie was Pavel's one and true love, and they had been so very happy. He had never considered that one day someone like Žofie would enter his world, but when she did, he had felt as if a long and unfinished puzzle had its final piece put in the right place to complete a perfect picture. The warnings of others had not made sense to him. He understood about anger. But not love. How could he be filled with such hope and possibility and have that love be something so catastrophic and wrong? Everything *was* perfect. The long years of extreme loneliness were worth every moment of his years of solitude and waiting.

They had been married for one week when Žophie sickened. Pavel was already one-hundred and seventy-three years old.

Pavel allowed the red-haired man with the familiar, yet strange eyes to lead him down the hospital corridor, away from Žophie, away from the doctors and nurses and sounds and smells. He needed to go back for her body. Arrangements needed to be made for her burial.

"I will help you with all of the arrangements that need to be made. You do not have to do this alone," McGovern said. They walked out of the hospital together into the front courtyard. The sun was shining in a brilliant blue sky. Rose bushes in full bloom lined the walkway that led from the doorway to the street. The roses seemed wrong to Pavel. Disrespectful and garish. The sun should not shine on a day when the entire light that was Žophie had been snuffed from the world.

"We should go to your home." McGovern guided Pavel by the arm. His hold was firm, but not rough.

"Did Mr. Trope send you, or did you come on your own?" asked Pavel.

"I was sent by Trope to keep an eye on you when you arrived. He anticipated there would be a problem. Actually, he anticipated there would be a disaster. We will have to send others to ensure that Žophie is the lone casualty.

Pavel did not fully comprehend what McGovern had said. Casualty?

"Will Cheidu be coming?"

"You mean Mr. Robert Lamb? Ah. Good. You do remember. That is good. A letter has been sent, and I'm sure your friend will be here as soon as he is able." McGovern did not sound convincing.

"You say I did this to her? To my Žophie? How could love do this? I was never angry. I was told never to get angry."

"You were warned about more than that. You ignored the letters from Mr. Trope. We tried to see you at every opportunity before you married and travelled here."

"I did not believe Trope. He is an insufferable man living his superior and distant life behind a desk. Do you know in all the years of our 'business' acquaintance we have never so much as shared a meal, as two regular people would? I endured his constant and rote statement telling me that things are 'in order' and 'when I am ready' and a lot more stuff and nonsense. Trope has never been in love. He could not possibly know."

McGovern squeezed Pavel's arm a little harder.

"That is a lie, and you know it. And you know nothing about Trope or what he may or may not have experienced during his life. You put your dislike of Trope above your common sense. But your best friend? How could you not listen to him? How could you be that selfish?"

Pavel wrenched his arm away from McGovern, and the two men continued to walk.

"Have you ever been lonely, McGovern? I think I asked you that once. A long time ago."

McGovern rubbed his gloved hands together and breathed deeply. "The fact you would ask that question of any of us proves that we have failed you. We should never have allowed you to stay in that theatre all those years. You have been sheltered like china doll in a cabinet. There is something wrong with you, with your mind. Over a century playing make-believe in a theatre where you have learned no concept of the real outcome of things—we are to blame for leaving you there. You have become a man without empathy, without consideration of anyone but yourself. Let's get you home. We should not speak of these things out in the open," said McGovern.

The two men walked in silence for a little more than an hour, the amount of time it took to walk from the hospital to the new home that Pavel had commissioned as Žophie's wedding gift. They walked up the stairs together and entered the foyer. McGovern took Pavel's hat and his and hung them both upon the rack that stood to the right of the door. He guided Pavel into the kitchen and into a chair at the kitchen table. Pavel watched as McGovern moved around the kitchen, lighting the iron range, putting the kettle on, opening cupboards and drawers until he found the teapot, the tea and the various cups and biscuits. McGovern picked an orange out of a bowl on the counter and peeled it, putting segments onto a plate that he found in another cupboard. He did not ask where anything was, and Pavel did not offer anything in the way of information that might help. Pavel sat in his chair and watched. McGovern seemed comfortable familiarizing himself with the kitchen as he put together their small meal.

Žophie had picked out the house's design from illustrations, and Pavel had made all of the arrangements with Mr. Trope's office to build the home, with some additional modifications of Pavel's design, namely the plumbing. Mr. Trope repeatedly protested the purchase and the move to America, but Pavel insisted. Mr. Trope's company took care of the house and travel arrangements while Pavel made separate arrangements on his own for his bride-to-be. He'd left Žophie's name out of the business arrangements, stating it was his desire to finally travel. He was not sure that Mr. Trope believed him or his deception. Pavel was counting on the fact that despite how Trope might feel about any given thing, his job was to keep his clients comfortable and happy. Pavel knew Trope & Co. would handle all the proper arrangements, whether or not the company agreed with its client. Pavel had promised Žophie's father he would take care of her in their new world. Pavel did not want to arrive in America at their new home and discover they had been swindled. One heard about such things happening. Trope & Co. arranged, over the course of several months, the purchase of everything pertaining to the home, including the furnishings and a business to keep the house clean until their arrival. While Trope handled all of the arrangements for the property's purchase, he continued to mail numerous letters to Pavel advising him against a continued association with his beloved. Pavel and Žophie said their goodbyes to friends and family and left for America immediately following the wedding, which was Žophie's plan and greatest desire. She was a forceful personality and did not take "no" for an answer. Her father was against the plan, as was Pavel, who had never lived anywhere else in well over one hundred seventy years. In the end both men relented.

On the long journey by ship, the newly married couple could not share a bunk because quarters were split between men and women. The wedding night they longed for would have to wait until they were in their new home. After what seemed to both to be a prolonged journey, they arrived in America, and dusty and dirty from travel, neither having had a proper bath for weeks, they approached their new house. No sooner had Pavel carried Žophie over the threshold of their brand new home when their hands and mouths were all over each other.

Pavel inhaled upon reliving the memory. Such a recent memory.

"I suppose without someone coming right out and stating their own experiences at tempting fate by living a normal life, you had no way of accepting, not without proof," James McGovern said, placing a plate of orange slices on the table. Pavel worried that this strange man could read his thoughts. "What I mean is, none of us truly knows unless there is an accident, and we tend not to speak of such things because they are terrible. Did it start with a bloody nose?"

Pavel was horrified by the man who asked if Žophie had gotten a bloody nose in the same tone that someone might ask if it had rained the night before.

"I did know," Pavel said. "I think I always knew. I wanted to forget. Žophie made me want to forget. Cheidu tried to talk some sense into me, but I thought that was because he—"

"Mr. Lamb is a homosexual, yes, but he was not trying to talk sense into you because he *desired* you."

Pavel slammed his hand on the table. McGovern gave him a stare that caused Pavel to immediately regret his outburst. He must control his emotions.

"I *know* that, you imbecile! Cheidu is my friend. My brother. Cheidu is my *only* friend and I am his. I thought maybe he did not want to be left alone. We were moving so far away, and he has had trouble here in America."

"None of us wish to be left alone. It is our circumstance in life to be creatures bound by hope for a connection. A lasting, human connection. For love. For something we cannot have and must not pursue," said McGovern.

Pavel considered the man's words.

"I mistook hope and love to mean the same thing. I honestly thought—"

McGovern rubbed his face with his hands. "It is our curse."

Pavel shook his head.

"I don't believe in curses. I believe in scientific explanations. When I was a small child they told me I had killed my family because I was some sort of demon. A vampire," Pavel said.

"There are no such things as vampires. We certainly don't go traveling around at night, sleeping by day in a coffin, drinking the blood of our fellow man. What a preposterous myth."

"I know that. But I have never understood how it is that we can be the cause of such destruction when we do not desire it? Which myth are we attached to? What is real?"

McGovern considered the question. He reached up and rubbed his shoulder, close to the spot where the scars would be that were identical to Pavel's.

"I have been called a changeling, a demon, a hobgoblin. I have read every book in Mr. Trope's office. The religious, the scientific— books do not explain *us*."

"Daoine Sidhe," said McGovern.

"Theena Shee?"

"Well, yes, that is how it is pronounced by the Celts and the Pagans. That's another name *I* have been called."

"What is that?" asked Pavel.

"A man-sized faerie sent to do all brand of mischief and steal souls. So some say. Others find them to be quite charming."

"I'm sure there are those that would find a vampire charming."

McGovern got up from the table and began searching around the cupboards until he found a block of chocolate and brought that back to the table and sat. He broke off a piece.

"How could you make yourself ignore all of Trope's letters? Did you dislike him that much?"

Pavel shook his head. "I don't know. When I was with my Žophie I could forget about everything else."

"But Mr. Lamb was there—"

"I told him to stop talking about it. He was my friend, so he did."

"You did have a family, though." McGovern got up again. He was highly agitated and began to pace the kitchen.

"Prochazka and Nina. My parents."

"Yes. The puppet maker and his beautiful wife."

"You say that like you knew them."

"Our paths crossed many years ago. First, when you were a child, and then when your father first brought you to meet Trope. You don't remember?"

"I suppose I do."

"Yes. They were good people. Kind people. And they loved you."

McGovern stopped pacing and faced Pavel.

"Perhaps that was our biggest mistake with you. Placing you with such exceptional people. Most of us do not have that. Perhaps that makes us more accepting of our nature. Too many years of creating make believe in your world, perhaps?" McGovern resumed his pacing.

Pavel was silent. He could not imagine a world other than the one Prochazka and Nina had created for him.

Pavel's eyes teared. "They didn't live very long either."

"Yes, I know. I was there. Contrary to what you might try to convince yourself, they lived the normal lifetime of normal people. But they were careful."

"*Normal* people."

McGovern's eyes searched Pavel's. "Žophie was also normal and subject to the same lifespan as other people. You would have seen her die after a normal, healthy life had she not been taken so abruptly. Had you done what your friend urged you to do and remained her friend."

Pavel whispered, "I fell in love with her. I could not let her go. I was going to. I thought of all the best ways to break it off. I couldn't. I loved her."

McGovern shifted in his seat and appeared to change the subject. "Are you religious at all, Pavel?"

Pavel seemed to remember this man, or someone, asking him that identical question. Who was it? It must have been a lifetime ago.

"You know that I am not. Don't tell me *you* are. I don't remember you being so."

McGovern regarded Pavel with scorn. "You choose to remember little. Some of us are. Perhaps I am. A little. Now. Not always. It is hard to live as long as we do and not adopt *some* sort of belief in something powerful over time."

Pavel stood and joined McGovern in pacing the kitchen.

"On the contrary. I have ascribed everything to the

natural sciences."

"Very well. As you know, some of us enter the clergy as a way of keeping to themselves. I suppose after a period of playacting at that, they begin to believe. Or the customs become a kind of comfort to them."

"Why would you adopt a belief in something that has others believing that you are something evil and that you should be killed? How many of us believe that we are angels of death sent by God who has tired of his creation? That's what Trope tried to tell me. We were sent here to do God's bidding? Get rid of the whole lot of this failed experiment called humankind?

McGovern stopped in his tracks. Pavel was in a dangerous mental state at present and had to be dealt with carefully.

"So, you do know. You never forgot."

Pavel made a disgusted noise that came out of the back of his throat like a gurgling rasp that made him cough.

"You don't honestly believe that? Do you feel this way as well? Because if you believe as they do, then you must think that of us. Are you here as my executioner today? Is our little conversation to precede my demise? If so, then please make sure that Cheidu gets everything, and try to come up with a good story for Žophie's family—why she died and why I was put to death."

McGovern shook his head. "You have seen many years in the theatre, Pavel. You are quite dramatic, I give you that. Your wife's father will be informed, by *you*, distraught as you may be, that she became ill during the voyage from Prague to America and that you put her immediately in hospital upon arriving here. As far as Eduard Rychtar will ever know, his daughter never arrived at her new home. The two of you never had the opportunity to act as husband and wife. There was no opportunity that could have resulted with her being with child before she became ill. The marriage was never consummated."

"Why is that important?"

McGovern got up again and moved to the drawers, opening and shutting them until he found pen and paper. He began writing.

"What are you doing?"

McGovern continued to write, ignoring the question, speaking as he went.

"Why is that important? Because if any of us is ever exposed it appears it would be due to you and your careless and unconscionable actions. You cannot appear to be in any way responsible for your wife's death. You had separate berths on the journey here. We need to make that separation extend to your getting off the boat, discovering she had taken ill during the journey and taking her to the hospital. There was no intimate contact. None. Do you understand? You cannot draw attention to the rest of us. We must protect ourselves."

"But I killed her."

"Yes, Pavel. Yes, you killed her."

McGovern handed the piece of paper to Pavel.

"What is this?

"This is the letter you have written to your wife's father explaining the tragedy of her death. Please read it and sign it in your hand."

McGovern glared at Pavel until Pavel took the pen, and with a weak hand, signed the paper, sliding it back across the table to McGovern. It was then that the reality of Pavel's actions seemed to sink in.

There was no exclamation from Pavel, no outburst. The entirety of him seemed to break and come apart when McGovern said those words. First his eyes went dead. The bluish swirl that moved and changed within his pupils went dark. All color left his face. Then Pavel seemed to crumple in upon himself, like one of his puppets left to sit in repose, each part of him collapsing upon the next part, hands and arms hanging limp, head dropping forward as if unsupported by his neck, legs askew as if not supporting any weight. The fact he did not slide off the chair and onto the floor surprised McGovern, who got up and put the kettle back on to reheat the water. He sat down again and faced Pavel across the table. The two sat like that for several hours. McGovern would get up after long intervals to freshen the tea, and Pavel did not once move. After several hours had passed, Pavel lifted his head with effort, as if his neck no longer supported the weight of his head, and he merely watched McGovern. Because of the falling darkness, McGovern had lit the lamps and come back to the table to wait.

"Drink this. It's fresh." McGovern put yet another cup of tea in front of Pavel, who did not take it.

"I'm going to give you some answers that will lead to more questions," McGovern said. "I ask for your respect and that you hear me out." Pavel said nothing. McGovern took a sip from his tea. He seemed to be considering his words.

"You appreciate the natural sciences. I do too. Imagine for a moment that there is a person who carries something physical in their blood or their liver, and that when that person is in a state of extreme passion, rage, for example, it spreads a sort of disease in a wave from the person while they are in that state and affects everyone in proximity. Is that something you can comprehend?"

Pavel made no indication he was listening.

McGovern shook his head. "How to explain something to someone who was so sheltered. It is obvious that living with people who kept you stimulated with those things that stretched your imagination and creativity, that your deeper passions were never compromised or fully ignited. We should have anticipated that."

McGovern got up again and began pacing. Pavel asked one question.

"If the person is a carrier of some sort of biological disease, then explain the wings."

McGovern stopped. "This is where I need you to be silent and hear me out."

Pavel kept his mouth shut.

"In ancient Egypt, students have found histories that have numerous stories of the god Ra, the Sun God. In one story, Ra becomes angry with his people, and decides to wipe them out. He sends winged children into the homes and temples of all his people to charm and enchant, but the winged children carry a terrible poison that will kill any and all who came in contact with them." Pavel's pupils remained dark and unresponsive.

McGovern continued to pace, his arms becoming more animated as he spoke.

"In Greek mythology, Zeus, God of the Heavens, becomes enraged with his human subjects one day and decides they should be destroyed, so he orders Hades, God of the Underworld, to kill all humans by sending winged demigod children into their midst who would play music on small flutes and harps that would lull the people into a permanent sleep. Hades, not wishing to have his Underworld overcrowded, puts a little wrench into the works. He removes the last remaining Virtue from Pandora's box— Hope. He renders Hope into millions of tiny pieces and places a piece into the heart of each of the winged demigods. This tiny bit of hope in each of them makes it impossible for them to see the humans as something that should be annihilated, and they put down their instruments."

Pavel seemed to stir at that. McGovern held up his hand to silence him before he could interject. His pacing increased.

"I mentioned the Daoine Sidhe from Celtic or Pagan mythology earlier, and the Pagans have creatures or beings or Gods and Goddesses for about every element that can be found in Nature, much like the Greeks; however, there is a darkness and a mischief to their gods, and they do not tolerate disrespect of any kind without some form of retribution. The punishment of humans for egregious acts by winged children was another variation. The Sidhe would replace a human child with one of its own to be raised by the humans. The winged child would come into the home and eventually poison the hearts of everyone in the house until they turned upon each other in acts of murderous rage."

"We have had nothing but time and years to study the various texts and apocryphal manuscripts attributed to many cultures. Ancient Babylonian gods who bring upon plague and destruction, rabbinic writings of the Jews in the Talmud,

Arabic writings, et cetera, all show references to some sort of angel of death, always a child with wings. One of the many lost books of the Bible depicts God, angry yet again and desirous of wiping out the entirety of his human creation, sending an angel of death in the form of a new infant to homes all over the globe. The child is born with the wings of an angel to fool the people into believing that they have been somehow blessed and are held high in God's favor. As soon as they kiss the baby, they fall into a poisoned and permanent sleep."

McGovern stopped his pacing, broke off another piece of chocolate and put it in his mouth, savoring it before he continued. He held the block of chocolate out to Pavel, who waved it away. Pavel sat expressionless. After so many hours, his exhaustion brought about by grief and extreme guilt caused him to shut down. His eyes went blank, the pupils no longer swirling, changing from blue to red and back to blue, but rather they remained deadened and black. He continued to listen to McGovern. He had no choice.

"My point is, Pavel, that there are too many similar legends from too many different places from too many religions that normally disagree with each other, sometimes with violence, yet they all share a story of winged children coming into their homes to destroy mankind after their God or Gods are angered by them. Every single one. It warrants attention."

Pavel hugged his arms to his body.

McGovern continued. "Alright, dismiss religion or mythology if you will. Let's consider science. Scientifically speaking, I am sure there would be no end of fascination and wonder about our kind, all the while dissecting and experimenting on each and every one of us. Cutting us open, weighing our organs, cutting off the top of our scalp to test regions of our brains with needles and probes, examining our veins to see if blood flows through them like other people. Religion and science are not so very different from one another. One kills over fear, one kills over curiosity. Which one is right? Either way, it is our belief that if discovered, we would be annihilated or worse, used for murderous purposes."

"You mean used as weapons?"

McGovern shrugged. His small physical action was almost dismissive.

"And how does Mr. Trope fits into all this? His leadership of the rest of us?" Pavel asked.

McGovern ignored the question and excused himself to use the privy, exiting the kitchen, leaving Pavel to sit in his spot at the table. Pavel briefly considered bolting out the door, to disappear forever and never come back but he dismissed the thought as soon as it entered his mind. He knew well that the others like him would have no problem locating him. Insertion into the lives of those like Pavel was their specialty. Pavel reached over and poured himself a fresh cup of tea, set it down, then rubbed his face vigorously to make himself more alert. They had been up several hours, and the conversation and circumstances were emotionally draining.

McGovern reentered the kitchen. "Ah, well, I see you haven't run away while I'm gone." Pavel looked stunned. Could McGovern read his mind?

"Mr. Trope deserves your respect, not your scorn." McGovern continued. "His offices are around the globe and their sole purpose is to protect our kind from discovery, and help our kind so that we do not resort to our baser nature. You ignored them and avoided them. You cannot blame Trope for this, Pavel."

Pavel considered McGovern's words.

"I have a question. We are supposedly bound by hope. We bring it to others and we are bound by it ourselves and that keeps us from acting out when impassioned."

McGovern waited for a question.

"Do you believe this idea come from the Greek myth? Is that where you believe this comes from?"

"Pavel, we live to be very old and there have been many of us along the way, philosophers, doctors, inventors, great minds that had years upon years to go back and forth examining our own natures. I guess you could say we did our own experimentation over time, without the torturous dissection. Yes, we researched similarities in all the mythology surrounding the winged children. The angels of death."

Pavel interrupted him. "The concept of hope was only in the Greek myth—the lost virtue."

McGovern rubbed his hand on his chin. They had been talking and sitting together for so long that red stubble was appearing on his face.

"I suppose you might find the belief to be quaint or romantic. But yes, we do believe, whether it came from self-examination over time, trial and failure resulting in disaster, or from some myth about Zeus and Hades, that each of us possesses the ability to access hope during times of despair and loss, and times of passion. It keeps us from acting on our original purpose. A sort of built-in defense mechanism, so to speak. We do believe our original purpose was the destruction of mankind. We do not believe that we are an accident of nature, or a scientific mutation. We believe we were born into the world very deliberately with that intention, by whomever or whatever pulls the strings, to use an analogy to your own profession. Infants have no impulse control, no way of knowing that their cries for hunger or to be held, or their rage because they dropped a toy, will cause plague or destruction. An infant child is the embodiment of passion. That is why so much death surrounds the birth of one of our kind. It is only if we live beyond that, that we can learn to control our baser nature and be something else. Most of us take years to study how to get very quiet within ourselves so that we do not become angry or passionate in any way.

Pavel considered that. His own upbringing had been about creating make believe, play, happiness for others. Prochazka and Nina had kept him in an environment where there would never be a reason to become overwhelmed by any extreme emotion. He experienced great happiness with them, but realized he never became impassioned to the degree alluded to by McGovern. Never to a degree that could cause harm. It was true. They had kept him like a china doll. Protected.

McGovern continued. "We have an ability by our proximity to others, to mortal people, to make them feel hopeful when we are near. Perhaps that is why Žophie was so taken with you, and her father so trusting. Perhaps it is why Prochazka and Nina were so instantly smitten with you upon your arrival on their doorstep. Mr. Trope's task, in his leadership, is to keep humans safe from us, while keeping us comfortable and content so that we do not become impassioned or enraged or vengeful about any one or more people. He protects *us*, because he does believe us to be sent by God or Gods. Mr. Trope and the people who work with him, like me, believe if the mortal population learned of our existence, we would be annihilated."

"They have already done their share of that," Pavel said with contempt.

"You mean the ones killed at birth? Yes, there have been so very many. Imagine evidence of gods that do not act randomly but in a calculated, vengeful manner. Mathematical even, if you factor in the location where some of us were born, our number and the timing of things. If the Church, if *anyone* were to find out, we would be hunted and destroyed. And as I mentioned before, Mr. Trope believes it might be worse than that. We might be used as weapons, which is a horrific thought."

"And Žophie?"

"Your passion for her. The act of making love. It weakens them. The gradual death starts with a bloody nose. The blood changes from red, thinning to violet and then to a pale matter similar in appearance to water. Whatever force is contained in the healthy blood dissipates to nothing of value that can sustain a life."

Pavel had been holding his teacup. When they began speaking of Žophie's death, his hand shook. He set the cup down with care. He did not want to break it. He had bought the set for her, though she would never drink from it.

"We thought our heads bumped. We laughed about it when her nose started to bleed. We *laughed*. I had no idea she was dying."

"I'm sorry," said McGovern.

"And I did kill my family and all those people," declared Pavel.

"Accidents occur. We try to ensure against them, that is all."

Pavel put his head down on the table. McGovern watched as Pavel closed his eyes. After a few minutes, Pavel fell into a deep slumber. The last pot of tea McGovern brewed contained Valerian root, which succeeded in putting Pavel to sleep. McGovern picked Pavel up and carried him to the parlor where he laid him upon a sofa. McGovern chose a chair across from him and settled in for a long, much-needed nap. His report to Mr. Trope would have to wait until tomorrow, but it was not his belief at that time that Pavel Trusnik had broken the Great Rule with deliberate malice.

Pavel would not be put to death.

Chapter 19

Kevin: Present Day

Kevin sat in the dark of the attic and watched out the window at the goings on in his neighborhood. The house across the street was dark. Kevin moved to the corner of the attic where he kept his tools. He opened the duffle and double-checked the contents: a length of rope, a hammer, and a set of lock picks he'd ordered off the Internet with the help of his parents, who thought he needed them for a school project. Kevin did write a paper about Internet privacy and used the lock picks as a visual aid when giving his oral report. He received an "A" grade. His duffle also contained a roll of chefs' knives and blister packs of ammonia inhalants for reviving the unconscious. Kevin did not want to be deprived of new music for his mp3 player in any way by the possibility his victim might go unconscious on him. He wanted his "instrument" to be awake and singing. The duffle also contained a small LED flashlight, a roll of plastic sheeting, surgical gloves, a surgical mask and safety goggles to protect his eyes. Kevin's scalpel and digital recorder remained tucked away in the front pockets of his jeans.

Kevin unrolled the blueprints one more time, though he had them memorized. He scanned the entry. Given the hour, the back door leading into the kitchen would be the easiest point of entry and was furthest from any rooms designated as bedrooms. He had taken great care in his attention to the details of every building addition or remodel to the home in the past thirty years and knew that there was no alarm system. The old guy had cable television, thought Kevin. He wondered if the old man was one of those people who liked to fall asleep in front of the television.

Kevin left the attic with his duffle. He moved down the stairs and past the door to his parents' bedroom where his mother slept on top of the covers. The bedroom television was turned on, volume low.

Kevin was about to descend the stairs when he heard his father's car turn into the driveway. He was supposed to be working late! Kevin sprinted to his bedroom, stowed the duffle under his bed and dived under the bedcovers, pulling them tight under his chin as he heard the back door open. He heard the sound of keys *clinking* into the bowl where his father tossed them when he got home. He listened to his father open the refrigerator and open something wrapped in foil. Kevin's father must have found something worth eating. He hoped it wasn't something that would involve cooking.

His father would often make omelets when he got home after a late night at work, and Kevin hoped that tonight would not be an omelet night. The slight tinkling of glass could be heard followed by the sound of the ice crusher on the fridge. Kevin's father was fixing a drink. Good. He almost never fixed a cocktail and an omelet on the same night. His father's footsteps came up the stairs, down the hall, pausing for a moment outside Kevin's door before continuing to the master bedroom.

Kevin waited for an hour until he was sure his father had finished his drink and was probably asleep next to his mother, on top of the covers, the television on. Parents are so predictable, he thought. He got out of bed, threw the covers back into place, grabbed the duffle and crept from his room, down the stairs, and out the back door. Then he sprinted to the house across the street. Everything was quiet.

Pavel watched the boy run across the street and through his garden. He knew he was moving toward the back door in the kitchen, where he now stood. People are foolish, he thought. And predictable. He opened the drawer where he kept the knives and selected one, then closed and locked the drawer. He took the magnetic child lock 'key' with him. No one else would be opening that drawer tonight.

He walked to the back workshop, checking various preparations along the way that he'd made earlier. He'd cut the main power to the house and moved in the dark, his oddly colored pupils shining. Whatever light he would choose to use would be powered by the auxiliary generator which was located in the workshop next to the kiln. The controller of the digital sound and light board was a small, handheld wireless gadget of his own design. He plucked it from the workbench and double-checked that it was powered and ready to go. He'd programmed the sound and lighting design—he was ready.

"Five minutes to curtain," he said aloud in the dark, as if he was a stage manager calling the cast together for a performance.

"Thank you, five minutes," he responded aloud to his own call to begin the show.

Chapter 20

1942

Pavel stood in front of his house, shaking with fury. "Where are your parents?" He faced the three boys who had sent a ball through his window, shattering the window and the framed photo on the wall directly opposite. He had run out of the house and, with the broken frame in one hand, he used his other to grab each boy before they could run, one by one, hard by the arm and pulled them into a tight group in the front of his house. He was enraged. Pavel held the ruined frame, glass broken, daguerreotype shattered, that had contained the sole photographic evidence of Her. If one stared hard enough at the broken daguerreotype, one could make out the line of a shoulder and a curl of what might be dark hair.

Pavel tried not to weep. His grief and anger were accelerating into something akin to rage and he was becoming overwhelmed by his emotional state. One boy, a skinny boy who looked like his arms and legs had grown too rapidly for the rest of his body, spoke up, voice shaken.

"Sorry, mister, it was an accident."

Pavel glared at him, furious.

"You hurt my arm," said another boy.

Pavel swung his head to stare down the next boy who dared speak.

"My father will pay for the window. Don't worry about it."

Pavel found his voice.

"Is that right? Your father can locate a window glazier today with access to 1880s vintage leaded glass? That is what was in there."

"Shut up, Stuart," said the first boy.

"Stuart, is it?" asked Pavel.

"Yeah, old man. It's Stuart."

"This was your idea, Stuart? There are baseball fields everywhere. Why would you play where you know you might cause damage? You have no idea what you've done."

"Yeah it was my idea. And it was a stupid window and a stupid frame. And you hurt my arm."

He slapped the boy full across the face. The other boys gasped. Stuart's nose bled, and he glared defiantly at Pavel.

Tears streamed down Pavel's face, his emotions no longer in his control.

"All of you need to leave here, right now. Never come back. Never play in this street again."

The boys gaped, jaws dropped, at the man who wept

in front of them, unsure of themselves or what to do.

"What do you want us to do about the window?" asked one of the boys.

Pavel wiped his face with his free hand, the other still clutching the frame.

"I will send the bill to your parents."

"You don't know who they are," said Stuart, wiping at his nose.

"I know who all of you are. I know where each of you live. Get out of here, now."

The boys ran.

Saturday's child works hard for his living, thought Pavel.

The man tried to think. Plans would have to be made. Arrangements.

The Great Rule had been broken. For that he would pay. He would pay dearly.

He walked with a certain amount of labor into his home, his emotional outburst having left him exhausted to the point where every muscle and sinew seemed to ache as if he had been dragged across the ground for a very long distance.

He would have to make a notification. Traveling anywhere was out of the question. He could not run. They would find him. Pavel thought of fleeing, but where would he go that he would not be found? There was a war on, and traveling to Europe was out of the question. Pavel walked into the kitchen and sat at the table, placing the frame on the table's surface.

He stood and moved to the counter and the black, Bakelite telephone. He picked up the receiver and dialed.

"This is McGovern," said the voice through the

receiver.

"McGovern, it is Pavel Trusnik."

"Yes, Pavel. What has happened?"

"I have broken the Great Rule."

There was a long silence on the other end of the line.

"Are you alone?"

"Yes."

"We will be over to take your statement. Please do not make plans to go anywhere."

"I won't."

"This is very serious, Pavel. It is important that you do not try to leave."

McGovern hung up, and Pavel stood for a moment, the receiver in his hand. He placed the receiver back in the phone cradle, and returned to the table and sat.

Pavel was terrified. He did not move. He would wait for McGovern.

He thought about McGovern, the large red-haired man. McGovern had always been kind to him. He had the hardened, thick-bodied appearance one might see in a police officer or fireman, and rumor had it that McGovern did consultations for the police from time to time. Despite McGovern's imposing appearance, Pavel knew him to have a compassionate nature. But would he now?

After an hour Pavel heard knocking on the front door. They can't have made it here already, he thought. The knocking continued. He crept into the living room and peered at the door and the two figures on the other side of the door's glass. He opened the door to Stuart with the man Pavel knew to be his father. Stuart held a bloody handkerchief to his nose.

"I'm Jim Jeffers. I believe you have met my son, Stuart. I understand that my boy broke your window today."

"Yes, that is true."

"You don't happen to know how my boy got a bloody nose from breaking your window, do you?"

Pavel sized up Jeffers. He was about Pavel's height, and a smattering of red veins decorated the surface of his nose and cheeks. A slight smell of alcohol on his breath explained the red veins. Pavel was too exhausted to enflame the emotions of a man who had been drinking. He kept his voice level.

"I'm afraid that I do. I slapped him. I'm sorry, Stuart." Pavel directed this last to the boy's face.

"You *slapped* him? Did he *say* something to you? Stu, did you *say* something to this man that he would *slap* you? People don't *slap* people unless they *say* something to get themselves *slapped*." The tone that Jeffers used with his son was disturbing.

"Sometimes boys can be impertinent if they are frightened. I'm sure Stuart was frightened after he broke the window," said Pavel.

"Is that what happened? My boy was *impertinent* after being *frightened*?" Pavel was not sure what was happening on his front porch, but he was growing more and more uncomfortable, both for himself and for the boy Stuart.

"I suppose," Pavel said. "How would you like to handle the matter of the window glass? It is the original glass from when the house was built. Leaded, 1880s. I'm afraid it is quite expensive." He met Jeffers' direct gaze and concentrated on making his expression as blank as possible.

Jeffers stared at him, his face growing red, his

breathing heavy, the smell of alcohol on him more obvious.

"I know the other boys were also responsible, so I'm sure some sort of arrangement can be made?" Pavel said.

Jeffers cleared his throat. Changing the subject to be about money had the effect Pavel had hoped for.

"I don't have the means right now."

"No one does, these days. I understand."

Jeffers stuffed his hands into his pockets. "We can board it up for you, until then."

"That will not be necessary. I can take care of that myself. I can also make arrangements to replace the glass and send you the bill to reimburse over time. Small payments. How does that sound?"

Jeffers said nothing, but seemed to consider Pavel's offer.

"Of course you would divide the bill among the families of the other boys responsible," Pavel suggested.

"Yes. Yes, I suppose that is fair."

"And I'm sure the boys will take their game to one of our many fields next time, yes?" Pavel glanced at Stuart, who glared back at him, and Pavel saw a glimpse of the boy he had slapped earlier that day. Pavel sighed.

Jeffers reached out his hand to shake on the deal. Pavel did not put out his hand. He had enough physical contact for one day. "I am expecting company soon, so if you do not mind, I need to get the window boarded up. It will be cold this evening."

Jeffers bowed his head and turned away from Pavel, shamed. He put his arm over his son's shoulders and steered him off the porch. Pavel stood in the doorway and watched as they walked down the street. Both father and son appeared to be broken. Pavel did not feel good about shaming Jeffers in front of his son over money, but it had to be done.

He did not wish to think about what was about to happen to Stuart. Pavel was familiar with what occurred when the Great Rule was violated.

Until that point of slapping Stuart, Pavel had never been forced to run, to move on, to start over. The periods in Pavel's life where he had moved from one group of people to another had been infrequent and happened either in an organic way or through careful organization on Pavel's part. Those moves carried little or no negative results. There was one... Pavel's mind wandered and he brought it back. Now this. The Great Rule had been broken, and Pavel must be patient and wait for McGovern to arrive. Pavel considered the consequences of his actions. He had heard rumors, but was unclear what would happen next.

Pavel boarded the window before McGovern arrived. He was not sure who else would be coming or how many there would be. He was certain that McGovern would be one of them. He tried to empty his mind of what was about to happen and concentrated on the task at hand. He moved to the back of his house to his workshop. He selected a measuring tape, went back to the window and measured, making sure to be precise with his selection of lumber and tools and cloths and cleaning supplies. Everything must be repaired with the utmost care. Pavel insisted upon keeping an immaculate home. He went back to his workshop and gathered the rest of the supplies. First, he cleaned the area in a deliberate and careful manner, sweeping up the glass, taking pains to ensure against scratching the pristine wood floor, leaving the broken glass that remained in the window so it might be easier for the glass company to find a match if they had a large enough sample to refer to. He scrutinized the area and determined that it was satisfactory, then got to work on boarding over the window. He was surveying his work on the outside of the house when he heard the small sound of gravel crunching under footsteps outside his house. He turned.

"Hello, Pavel," McGovern said. McGovern held a satchel at his side that was stuffed with papers. He was with two other men. One man appeared to be on the young side, olive-skinned, dark hair, maybe in his twenties, though Pavel knew that appearances were unreliable. The other had a rather Nordic appearance to him: tall, blonde hair that was turning white, and close to middle age. Again, Pavel knew that was an unreliable judgment, since both he and McGovern appeared to be middle aged and were most certainly not. That was their nature.

"This is Revera." McGovern indicated the young man. "And you may remember Peters." he pointed at the older man. Both bowed their heads in somber greeting.

"McGovern. Gentlemen. Please come inside."

The four men walked up the steps to Pavel's home and went through the door. Pavel peered outside at the street before shutting the door.

McGovern, Revera and Peters followed Pavel into his home. Pavel had never heard of anyone actually breaking the Great Rule, and he was not sure of the punishment involved when one did so. He had the impression that the punishment was particular to the person who had committed the offense. That did not comfort him. He led the men through the house.

"Would you prefer the living room, or the kitchen? I can serve you tea in the kitchen."

"The kitchen will be fine." They walked past the front room and the living room where the furniture was covered with sheets. The house appeared to have been shut up either for a sale or for a time while the owners were away.

"It doesn't appear that you use much of the house," Peters said.

"Not much reason to," said Pavel. He led them into the spacious kitchen and indicated that they should select where they wanted to sit at the table. He set out food on plates for snacks and put on a kettle for tea.

The three men chose seats at the table while Pavel continued playing host to this strange trio. Of judges. He breathed to calm himself and attempted to remain neutral.

"Unless anyone would prefer coffee? I think I might have some."

"I'd like some," Revera said.

McGovern shot Revera a look.

"Tea will be fine," McGovern said.

Revera shrugged his shoulders, but did not argue. Once Pavel had everything on the table and arranged in front of the men, he took a seat and joined them.

"Well then, shall we begin. How bad is this?" Pavel asked.

"Speaking in the strictest of terms," Peters said, "this is your second offense, the first of course, being your wife."

"But I—" said Pavel.

"You're going to have to stay quiet on this and hear us out," Revera said.

McGovern reached into the satchel at his side on the floor and brought out a mountain of paperwork. He handed the paperwork to Peters. Peters consulted something on one of the sheets and spoke without looking at Pavel.

"The first offense was your wife. Your repeated warnings from Trope & Co., not to mention your own friend, Mr. Robert Lamb, are an indication that people attempted to warn you that your association with Miss Rychtar could prove dangerous, yet you chose to not heed those warnings," said Peters.

McGovern spoke up. "You were forgiven and went unpunished when I came to you after Žophie died. That was determined to be a tragic accident, based in large part, to our lack of forethought in having you raised in an environment that left you unprepared for a more reality-based world. This, however, is the second time for you, when your impulse has overridden your common sense of whom and what we are. The boys are sick. The boy you slapped is deteriorating. In order to shield you and by association, us, we have arranged a short-lived epidemic that will not only affect the boys, but people in the surrounding areas and scattered locations beyond that. That solution is unavoidable. The disease is a common flu, but as you know, the flu can spread to many people."

Peters slid a sheet of paper and a pen over to Pavel who was so nervous he could not read what was on it.

"Sign it," said Peters. "It is an acknowledgment that your actions required taking extraordinary steps to avoid attention and discovery and that you are aware of and agree with these steps."

Pavel was horrified. "But many people could die," he

said, his face draining of any remaining color.

"Yes. Many people will die because of your actions. This is why we take certain precautions with respect to our interaction with others," said Peters, holding the pen out to Pavel.

"But how can you do this? They are innocent people!"

Revera made an exasperated sigh. "So was your wife. So were those boys." He switched his focus from Pavel to McGovern. "I'm going to make some coffee, if that is all right with you."

McGovern glared at him for a moment, then made a gesture of assent with his hand. Revera got up and found the tin of coffee in the cupboard, put on a pot to boil water and stood at the counter, watching the others. Revera focused his attention on Pavel and continued from his place at the counter.

"You grabbed each of the boys in a rage. You slapped one. He will die before the others because your rage was directed more at him. Their blood will be water in a matter of hours, perhaps a little longer. You were the last person to have contact with them. Attention will, as a matter of course, fall to you."

McGovern continued, taking his cue from Revera. "In order to draw attention away from you, it must look like the three boys were exposed to the same flu. A flu that many will get, starting today and stretching into the next few weeks until it runs its course through everyone infected by it."

Revera measured coffee into the now boiling water and continued where McGovern left off. "It has already started. This is the sort of thing we are trained to do, and we are very good at it." Revera said. Pavel's heart began to flutter.

In the short time allowed before arriving at Pavel Trusnik's home, Revera walked with determination down a path through the park on Raymond Avenue in Pasadena. He carried a newspaper in his hand. He took off his heavy gloves, stuck them in his pocket, then ran his bare hands in a methodical manner, taking care to touch every part of the paper, getting newsprint on his hands in the process. He deposited the newspaper on one of the park benches. He approached a woman walking with two toddlers.

"Excuse me, ma'am?"

"Yes?"

"Can you tell me how to get to Euclid Avenue from here?" At that moment, one of the toddlers tripped on the path and fell down. Revera immediately bent down and picked up the toddler. He handed the toddler to the woman, brushing her hand when doing so. The toddler began to cry.

"Never mind. I'll ask someone else. You are rather busy. Thank you, though."

Revera walked away from the woman, looking behind him in time to see a man sit on the bench where he had left the paper. He watched the man pick up the paper and begin to read.

Meanwhile, McGovern and Peters were in other public areas that radiated out from the street where Pavel Trusnik's house was situated. Each came in contact with a handful of people, either on a streetcar or in the library, or in other places where the public might gather. Each man left behind a book or a toy that would attract the attention of someone who might pick up the object to inspect it or to hand it to someone else.

Each of these people would fall ill with the flu later that day and in turn would pass it along to someone else. Some of those people would travel to other parts of the city or get on a train and travel even further, and the flu would spread. Some would recover; some would die. The three boys that Pavel had manhandled that day would be among the number that did not survive.

"But to kill all of those people?" Pavel asked.

"You killed three innocent boys today. Are you attempting to judge? The Rules exist so that people do not die indiscriminately and that horrible accidents are prevented as much as possible. You have treated the Rules with alarming negligence and placed us all in this position.

"What is my punishment?" Pavel asked, his eyes wet.

"You are given a choice. It is up to you which one you decide upon. The first and most obvious choice is death. You are put to a sudden and painless death, thus ending any possibility of your actions affecting others or our safety ever again. Your other option, which some of us are against, is for you to be placed under house arrest for the remainder of your natural life. You are to remain here and have no interaction with another person. You may contact members of Trope & Co. for the maintenance of your home and affairs by telephone and post. You are to arrange delivery of all your other needs. If maintenance must be done on your home, you are to arrange workmen by telephone and by post. You must remain inside. You may go into your garden at night, never during daylight hours, and you are to remain behind the fence. You are not to venture into the city under any circumstances. You are to be shunned by our kind and you will have no contact with us, other than the maintenance we have already mentioned. You will suffer a particular kind of solitary confinement, but with the comforts of home. That is your second choice."

Pavel regarded his hands as he searched for answers that would not come. He recalled a similar moment many years ago when he had looked for answers in the nail beds of his fingers. Answers did not come then either.

Peters spoke up. "Keep in mind that whatever arrangement you choose may last for a very long time, and solitary confinement is a serious sentence. Many go mad. It is, of course, an alternative to death."

Pavel and McGovern regarded one another. McGovern spoke up.

"Pavel, you and I know that you have not handled this level of solitary existence well in the past. You did go mad for a time, and there were people around you. This time, there will be no one. No drugs created from your garden as a means of mental escape. We cannot stop you from ordering liquor in your grocery delivery, but that will be all. Nothing more. No visits from us. You and I will not be having tea."

Pavel understood. What he could not explain to them was that he felt his actions warranted a more severe punishment. Putting him to a sudden and painless death was no punishment. Too merciful. The consequences had to be worse than that.

"And if I do not succeed in following the rules of the second arrangement? If I break the rules of solitary confinement and have contact with another person?"

McGovern searched Pavel's face. "The punishment for breaking the rules of sentencing is very harsh because it is meant to make a point, to serve as an example to others who might follow in your path." McGovern answered Pavel's questioning gaze. "We burn you alive."

Pavel flinched. Death by fire. The way they had done away with so many of his kind during the years surrounding his birth was somehow fitting. Pavel pulled the paperwork to him, read it briefly and then signed his name to it. McGovern and he exchanged a look a moment before McGovern averted his gaze. The men got up from the table, gathered the signed agreement and filed out of Pavel's house, leaving him alone. His sentence had begun.

Chapter 21

Pasadena, 1950

Pavel had been drinking, which was not his custom, but he had been drinking more often in the past decades. He had been a widower for over sixty years, the number of years most happy marriages last—those granted the gift of a lifetime together, that is, before one is lost to the other by the cruelty of a natural death that always leaves one alone, mourning the loss of the other. Pavel spent many an evening alone in his workshop, drinking, carving wood, talking to the many puppets he'd shipped in crates from Prague when he had emigrated to America.

This particular evening Pavel was a bit more drunk than usual. He was weeping. He wiped his hand across his face and moved in an unsteady line to a large cabinet built into the wall. He took a skeleton key from around his neck, unlocked the cabinet, reached in and with great care, removed one life-sized marionette controlled with rods and wires. This puppet wore a long gown of silver blue silk and lace. The carved face looked up at him, unblinking.

Pavel stroked the face of the marionette he held in his arms. He draped one puppet arm over his shoulder and took the other hand in his own and in a slow and languid waltz rhythm, began to dance around the room. The puppet dangled, limp in his arms.

"Ah, dear Juliet, why art thou yet so fair? Shall I believe that unsubstantial death is amorous, and that the lean abhorred monster keeps thee here in dark to be his paramour?" Pavel continued reciting Romeo's last words to Juliet, in a close embrace. "For fear of that, I still will stay with thee, and never from this palace of dim night depart again: here, here will I remain with worms that are thy chamber-maids." Pavel hugged the marionette and sobbed.

"O, here will I set up my everlasting rest, and shake the yoke of inauspicious stars from this world-wearied flesh. Eyes, look your last!" His eyes sought a reaction from the marionette, and when that reaction never came, he continued a waltz-like dance around the room. "Arms, take your last embrace!" Pavel lifted both the limp arms up and over his shoulders into a macabre hug. "And, lips, O you the doors of breath, seal with a righteous kiss a dateless bargain to engrossing death!" Pavel brought the puppet to him for a one-sided embrace as he kissed the carved face of the unmoving marionette. "Come bitter conduct, come unsavory guide! Thou desperate pilot, now at once run on the dashing rocks thy sea-sick weary bark. Here's to my love!" Pavel swung her around, and with one hand, picked up the bottle from which he had been drinking and tipped it to his lips.

The sound of clapping startled him.

"Who's there?"

"Here's one, a friend, and one that knows you well," said a voice, reciting the character Balthasar.

Pavel shook his head to clear his vision which was altered by the amount he'd been drinking. A tall black man was approaching him in the darkness from across the room. Could it be his old friend? It was not possible.

"Cheidu?"

"You said your door was always open to me and I took you at your word." The man moved closer to him in the dark and studied him. "Hello, my dear old friend."

Pavel was confused. Robert Lamb was here? He could not be here. It was forbidden.

"Cheidu? Is it you? How can you be here? You are not supposed to be here." Pavel's words slurred a bit.

The tall, well-dressed black man walked in a tentative manner around the workshop which resembled a miniature version of the one where Pavel had spent his days in Prague, with the same ordered arrangement of shelves, pegs, hangers, tools. How many years had it been since Cheidu had stood for the first time in that other doorway?"

"They have these things called automobiles that have made the most astounding advances over time. They are quite... flashy, I think is the right word," said Robert. "But that is not what you meant by your question, is it?"

Pavel stumbled a little and righted himself against the worktable, clutching the puppet to his body.

"I want you to know that I tried to come. I was on my

way here. Would you believe I was arrested and sent to prison for stealing my own car? The court threw the proverbial book at me. They made a decision that the proof I offered, that the car was indeed mine, was forged. Falsified. They concluded a man like *me* couldn't possibly afford a car like *that*. They did not like the way I speak." Cheidu slipped into a perfect impersonation of the dialect of a white southern man. "You sure don't talk like your kind—where did you learn that?" He went back to using his own voice. "It turns out they did not appreciate that my level of education and breeding exceeded their own. They decided that I *must* be a criminal or at the very least a skilled con man and a stolen car was more than likely the least of my numerous imaginary offenses they could prove. So. My dear friend. I have been in prison. For thirty years."

Pavel, confused, said nothing.

"I tried to see you," Robert continued. "I tried to get the gentlemen at Trope & Co. involved in my release. Would you believe they said that they could not help? They said it was best if I disappeared for a while—that people like me were more difficult for them to keep at a low profile. I am an actor! What actor keeps a low profile?! They assured me that when I came out they would give me new papers with a new name." Robert searched his silent friend's face.

"What do you think of the name Cedric Lamb, descendant of the great stage actor, Robert Lamb? I can do movies now!" He bowed low for his friend. There was still no response from Pavel.

"There was something further. The gentlemen at Trope & Co. forbade me to see you. Something about you being under 'house arrest' and shunned? Are they serious?

They let me, a *'negro,'* sit in an American prison for thirty years and tell me I cannot see my oldest friend?"

Lamb, making slow and careful steps, moved closer to Pavel.

"Though it seems I have found you at a bad time. May I say though that I had no idea you knew the role of Romeo quite so well. Quite moving. And who is playing the fair maid Juliet in tonight's pageant?"

Pavel pulled the puppet tighter against him and stumbled back to the cabinet from where he'd removed it.

"Pavel. I have heard rumors that my old friend has not been doing very well. That your emotions may be hurting you. That something may be happening to your mind."

Pavel stumbled and tried to focus his vision on his friend. "They told me some who make my choice often go mad. Should I have chosen fire?"

Lamb looked stricken.

"I wanted to get here sooner, my friend. I did try. A man of my complexion has difficulty traveling in America. Still. I had such high hopes that by now things might be different, but alas, I am as always, ever hopeful, yet quite deluded. Imagine that. It has taken me too long to get to you. Decades long. With egregious living conditions along the way. Remind me never to travel through any part of the south in this country."

Pavel struggled to open the cabinet. Cheidu approached him.

"Let me help my old friend with that." Cheidu reached out and opened the cabinet door. He glanced inside and took an immediate second look and gasped. He turned and looked down at the puppet in Pavel's arms.

"Pavel. What have you *done*?"

"She's gone, Cheidu. She's gone. My Juliet is gone."

Pavel sank down to the floor, cradling the puppet in his arms. The dress hiked up to reveal skeletal feet and legs beneath. Robert Lamb pulled the dress up higher to reveal more of the skeleton. He admired the artistry in the carved wooden replica of such a familiar face. Žophie's face. Pavel sat there, limp and crying, his hands at his sides. Robert Lamb removed the wig and found the place where the wood mask met with another material. He lifted the mask off a pristine white skull. He laid the wig and mask upon the floor, next to the skeleton dressed in silver blue silk and lace.

"I'm going to ask you again, Pavel, what have you done?"

"I couldn't put her in the ground. I couldn't leave her. I wanted her with me. I *need* her with me."

"And Prochazka?"

Pavel faced his friend, tears streaming down his face. "And Máma."

Cheidu, devastated, questioned his friend. "What has happened to you?"

Pavel ran his hands through his hair, then clutched them together at his chest, then put them out before him in a pleading gesture. "Prochazka always said that the goal when building a puppet was to make the joints function in the same way of a real human skeleton. So, think about it, Cheidu. It is logical. If you use the actual bones, *all* the bones, you can make a very realistic moving marionette."

"Oh, my God. Pavel."

"Funny. You using the word, 'God,' my old friend. Very funny, indeed."

"Help me understand this."

"*I was lonely!*" Pavel cried with surprising volume and noticed the skeleton sprawled on the floor. "No! We can't leave her like that. We have to put her back."

Cheidu began to weep.

"Pavel, that was Žophie. Your Žophie. She deserves a proper burial."

"My Juliet."

"I understand. Your Juliet. You were star-crossed. You and your Juliet were never meant to be. You think I, of all people, don't know that? Who understands such things more than me, Pavel? Who? I know. I have loved as deeply as you have loved. But I *never* acted on that love. None of us can. Neither of us was destined to have what our own natures cruelly desired for us. I know and you knew, my dear friend. You *knew* such a union could and would end in tragedy. But you *hoped*, didn't you my friend? That is what we do. We *hope*. And sometimes we hope for the worst of all possible things. I know that is what happened to you, Pavel. I know. I understand."

"I *never hope!*" shouted Pavel.

"We are not ghouls. This is wrong. I need to contact the others. We can help you."

"No. No, I can't let you do that. They will take her away again."

"My dearest friend, Pavel, let me help you. I can't watch you go mad in front of me. Please. Let me help you." Cheidu moved to stand. He was almost upright when Pavel, still on the floor, in an impulsive act of desperation, pulled Cheidu's legs out from under him. The tall man came down, throwing out his arms to break his fall, but he fell backwards.

His hands could not catch hold of anything that might help him. His head struck the sharp corner of the worktable. The sound of skull and brain matter smashing against the solid wood had an instant sobering effect upon Pavel.

"Cheidu?" Pavel moved to his friend, on the floor, who was not moving. Cheidu's eyes were open, startled.

"Cheidu?"

Chapter 22

Present Day

Pavel sat in the dark workshop and through the window reflection watched Kevin come in through the kitchen door. He slowed his breathing, though adrenalin was beginning the familiar rush that preceded every stage performance he remembered.

Pavel checked his control board and microphone. He glanced at the digital clock on the wall. He put down the control board and climbed a ladder which led to a narrow window near the ceiling, where he could see across the street to Kevin's house. He watched McGovern and two other men stride up the walkway toward the front door of Kevin's house. He released a sigh of resignation.

It was time. He had to come down off the ladder.

McGovern's presence with the others meant there were more characters to introduce to the play. He moved down the ladder with the nimble confidence and speed of someone who had spent years of his life going up and down ladders.

"Curtain," he said. He picked up his portable control board and fiddled with a couple of levels. Pavel sat back in the dark and waited.

Kevin padded through the kitchen like a cat hunting a small sparrow. He attempted opening a drawer and felt a slight electrical shock when he put his hand upon the knob, which did not open. He shook his hand to get rid of the residual tingling effect from the slight shock. He then tried a cabinet, but the child locks held so that the drawers and cabinets did not budge. There would be no souvenirs. "Weird," Kevin said aloud. He noticed the smell of vinegar and furniture polish, but noticed another smell. The smell reminded him of a wood shop: melted soldering wire and the odd, metallic smoky odor of an active soldering iron. And epoxy resin. Perhaps Mr. Trusnik liked to tinker. His thoughts were interrupted by a voice.

"Hello, Kevin." The voice came from directly behind him. Kevin whipped around, but there was no one there. The empty and dark kitchen was illuminated by the moonlight that came through the windows. Kevin turned back around, and the sound of barking started again, this time behind him and a little to the left. What appeared to be a *puppet* of a small poodle went clicking by on the floor, dancing. The lights came up a little bit, enough to make the room brighter on the area where the poodle was doing its odd dance.

"What the fuck?" Kevin asked. The lights went out, and he could no longer see the poodle. Kevin patted his pocket to assure himself that the scalpel was there, but put down the duffle bag. There was something weird in this house, and he might need use of both of his hands. He crept from the kitchen and into the darkness of the hallway as an abrupt spotlight came on, illuminating a skeleton dancing directly in front of Kevin's face, its bones rattling. The spotlight was extinguished, and the skeleton was gone.

"Hello, Kevin." The voice came from his right, as if someone was talking into his ear. He threw out his arm, but nothing was there.

Kevin smiled. He was in the house of a game player. "Oh, Mr. Trus-nik," called Kevin, in a sing-song voice. "Looks like I came to the house of someone who digs Halloween."

"How many people have you killed, Kevin?" The voices filled his left ear and something brushed against him, something sharp.

"Ow, *fuck*," said Kevin. He reached with his free hand to inspect his arm, discovering a small cut there. Blood came away on his fingers. The lights came up again on the rattling skeleton in front of him which waved a knife and shook as if laughing, though the sound of the laughter came from somewhere behind him.

"What the f—"

"How many people have you killed, Kevin?" asked the voice. The lights went out on the rattling skeleton.

"You don't frighten me, you old freak," said Kevin.

"Who is in whose house right now, uninvited?" asked

the voice which came from a corner off to Kevin's right. "You have the blueprints." A follow spot faded up to light the end of the hallway, but the spot was focused on an empty floor. "Were the blueprints informative?" The voice was right behind Kevin. He whipped around again as the dog barked, ran in front of Kevin and tripped him in the dark. Kevin fell to the floor and screamed in pain. In the dim light, he brought his hand to his face. His hand was caught in an animal snare with pieces of razor wire wound through the snare. The wire bit into the flesh of his hand.

"I'll fucking kill you!" Kevin screamed.

"Oh, I don't think so, Kevin. You see, people who get near me are the ones who end up dead. How many people have *you* killed, Kevin?" The spotlight lit up the skeleton yet again, which danced in front of him. The skeleton held up its hand, this time revealing a small digital recorder. The light went out and the skeleton disappeared, making a rattling sound like that of a gigantic wind chime. Kevin reached down with his good hand to feel his pocket. His recorder was no longer there. How did he…?

"How many people have you killed?" The voice seemed to be directly over Kevin's head this time.

"What? You're going to get me to confess to something and then what?" Kevin listened in the dark, but there was no response from the voice.

"Who would you give it to, old man? You never leave here, I know that."

The voice piped up behind him. "Have you heard of the Internet?"

Kevin tried to move his head in the direction of the voice, but was constricted by his awkward position on the floor. He was going to have to find a way to get up.

The disembodied voice spoke again, and this time it seemed to come from the end of the hallway, beckoning. "How often do you think they will replay this video on the evening news?" In the dark, Kevin saw a small red light, like that on a video camera, but he was having difficulty deciding the precise location *where* it was in front of him. The pain in his hand distracted him, and the lights kept changing, messing with his field of vision.

"How do you know my name?" Kevin asked.

"You seem to know mine. We're all old friends here. And you have met my father, yes?" The skeleton plopped down next to Kevin as if in a squatting position and reached out for the snare on Kevin's hand. Kevin batted at the skeleton but never made contact with it, for it immediately rose up and out of his field of vision. Kevin felt very strange. His adrenalin should have been pumping through his body, causing his pulse to quicken, his peripheral vision to expand. Instead, things seemed to be slowing down for him. He could feel his heart thudding in his chest like a metronome set at a very slow rhythm.

"Did you poison me? When you cut me?"

"Oh, heavens no. I don't have to do that. I can't speak for the escaped puppets, however. They do enjoy experimenting with herbs. Did you know my father was an escaped puppet? They tried to lock him in a tomb," said the voice.

"You're insane!" said Kevin as he felt his heartbeat quickening, followed by a flush to his cheeks and ears. He was experiencing that rush of adrenalin, though the feeling was not what he was accustomed to having during one of his experiments with a subject. The fight-or-flight phenomena urged him to run but simultaneously paralyzed him. He was unable to scream, to move. He took a deep breath and tried to suppress this new experience, which would not serve his purpose today. *Is this what fear feels like?* he thought.

"Oh heck. I'm an old man, a shut-in who could not possibly defend himself against a boy like you. How old were you when you killed your first human?"

"You poisoned me!" Kevin tried to struggle.

"I'll tell you how old I was. I was a newborn child. That birth caused the death of over ten thousand people. I win." That last was delivered sing-song, taunting. The words "I win" seemed to come from all around Kevin and reverberated off the walls.

"I'm going to the cops about you. I'm injured. I need help. You drugged me."

"How many people have you killed, Kevin. I'll make it easier. How many this year?"

"Shut up!" Kevin yelled.

"Okay, too difficult? Too many to remember?"

"The thing is," the voice said to Kevin, this time coming from his right, as if someone was seated next to him on the floor, "when those people died I did not wish them harm. I took no pleasure in it."

Kevin started to crawl forward. He made it ten more feet, closer to what appeared to be a door at the end of the corridor. A net dropped over him, tangling him into an immobilized heap on the floor.

"You fucking fuck! You cocksucker, I will fucking kill you!" Kevin yelled as he writhed and further tangled himself in the netting.

The voice chuckled. "My father liked to swear. It always made me laugh." Music started from somewhere deep in the house. Chopin's *Minute Waltz*. If Kevin squinted through the netting, he could make out what appeared to be the skeleton dancing with a marionette of a woman, waltzing in time to the music, both controlled by an unseen puppeteer. They seemed to be at the end of a corridor but then, in the next instant, appeared quite close to him. Kevin's vision was playing tricks on him. He stopped struggling. He had to figure out a way to get out of the net.

"Meet Máma, another escaped puppet," said the voice. "My parents loved me very much. Do your parents love you, Kevin?"

Kevin felt with his good hand to see if his scalpel was still in his pocket. It was. He fished it out, and brought it to his mouth, using his teeth to release it from its square of leather. Kevin started slashing at the net to escape.

"Oh, tsk," said the woman marionette, who was somehow suddenly next to him on the floor. "I think you had better answer my son's question, Kevin. How many people have you killed?" The marionette leaned over him, her hands on her hips, accusing, eyes unblinking.

"My mother does not want me to hurt you," said the voice. "None of them do."

"None of who? Your stupid puppets, Mr. Trusnik?" asked Kevin.

"Oh, I assure you they are much more than that. No, I mean the others. The men at your house who are searching your room right now."

"What?"

"And the attic. Attics in old houses are always such

good places for hiding things, don't you think?"

"Who *are* you?" asked Kevin.

"They don't want me to kill you. That is what they are attempting to prevent. They are trying to stop an event from occurring. Can you give me a reason why I should not kill you?"

"Fuck you." Kevin was quite frightened. The cocky confidence he had when he broke in and his intentions against Mr. Trusnik were gone. All he wanted was to get out of there.

"Let's start with why you are here."

"Let me see you!" yelled Kevin, forgetting his resolve to remain calm. He struggled again with the netting.

"What was it that you planned on doing to me when you got into my house? Assuming I was the defenseless shut-in you were expecting."

"Come out of the dark, old man. Enough with the puppet show. Who is searching my house?"

"One of my associates. Accompanied by the police, I should expect."

The police. Kevin had not counted on any of this. Everything had been so perfect, so planned.

"They won't find anything."

"I told them to check your mp3 player first."

"You son of a cocksucking *bitch*. That is *mine*!" Kevin was furious. He could not believe his ears. How had the old man known about his music?

"Ah. Struck a chord. People don't *like* having their personal space and privacy violated. End of first lesson. How does it feel?"

"Get me out of this net and I won't kill you." Kevin's

speech was slurred. He heard a chuckle which seemed to come from multiple directions.

"Oh. You won't kill me. But how many have you killed?"

"Stop saying that!"

The lights blinked on and off from different locations, as the music faded from one location to get louder in another, repeating in a maddening loop that disoriented Kevin further. He felt as if he'd happened upon a haunted house and at any moment something would jump out at him from anywhere. His vision was blurred and his muscles were not reacting. He felt defenseless. Was this how they felt? His experiments?

The poodle ran by, barking while a voice repeated, "Meet my parents. They are escaped puppets. Meet my parents. They are escaped puppets. Meet my parents. They are escaped puppets." The skeleton and female puppet twirled and danced in the hall. Kevin thought he was going mad.

As a light blinked overhead, Kevin glimpsed a metal track in the ceiling, over where the puppets were waltzing.

"I know how you're doing your stupid tricks. I can see the track, you fucker!"

"Tsk. You see? No matter how sophisticated the design, it is always possible to spot the mechanics if one looks hard enough. To see the magician's hand, so to speak. So what will they hear on your mp3 player, Kevin?"

Kevin's efforts paid off. He burst through the netting and used his foot as leverage to pry apart the animal snare that held his hand. Kevin screamed when he opened the snare, and his hand throbbed in pain. His blood that seeped from the puncture wounds seemed to be an odd color, a sort of pale violet. Watery. His head felt heavy, and he wondered if his neck could support the weight of it. Kevin got to his feet and stumbled down the hall, deeper into the house. He used the wall for support as he went, but sections of the wall seemed spongy, as if they were made of fabric. His hand sank into the wall until it stopped at something hard and cold. He kept going, holding his good hand with the scalpel out in front of him.

Kevin, half crawling, half stumbling, worked his way toward the end of the hall and then turned in the direction of the music. His breath came in short bursts. He remembered a vacation to New Mexico with his family once, and the altitude had made him breathe this way for a short time until he got used to it. Why did he think about that vacation now? The music became louder as he approached a doorway at the end of another short hall built at a right angle to the one he was navigating at present. He approached the door and opened it.

The door opened upon a huge workroom, filled with tables and tools. Are those puppets? Kevin asked himself, seeing marionettes hanging from hooks on the walls and dangling from the ceiling like some sort of creepy slaughterhouse hung with hundreds of dolls. Inside the huge room was an old man, wearing a cardigan, dancing with a marionette of a woman in a silver-blue gown. The old man did not stop dancing upon Kevin's entrance. The music grew louder, and the lights changed to a random display of locations and levels of illumination, some bright, some a dull glow, some glaring into his eyes, which gave Kevin spots in his line of vision.

Kevin stumbled into the room, held the scalpel in front of him and crept toward the old man who seemed unaware of Kevin's presence. A booming voice directly behind Kevin bellowed, "How many people have you killed, Kevin?" He lurched around as fast as his present muddled state would allow and standing before him was an enormous puppet of a black man in bright colored robes. When the puppet moved, it made the same sort of rattling, wind-chime noise that Kevin had heard from the skeleton puppet. Kevin lunged at the puppet with his scalpel, and the puppet danced to the side and out of his way.

"Now is that any way to behave?" asked the puppet. "I can't have you coming in here, trespassing, with the intention of harming my dear friend over there. He has had a rough time of it, you see." The puppet slid back and away from Kevin, on a track that ran on a grid installed in the high ceiling.

"You're not real! He is doing all of this!"

Kevin heard Mr. Trusnik speak. "I had so hoped we would not have to meet in person. In the same room. I had hoped it would not get this far. People are so very foolish. Don't you find them to be foolish, Cheidu?"

The puppet of the black man moved forward again, then switched direction and moved closer to Mr. Trusnik. "Without question, people are foolish," it seemed to respond.

"Stop doing that!" yelled Kevin as he slashed out with the scalpel but met with dead air.

"Not a lover of theatre, it seems," said the puppet.

"No. It would seem not," responded the old man.

"So few of the young people are these days," said the puppet. "They would rather be at the movies, or in front of a television or computer."

"I agree. It is a sad state of affairs," the old man agreed.

Kevin felt like his muscles were starting to fail.

"What did you drug me with?" said Kevin.

"A little something to help you sleep. It was my intention to get you out of here and onto the front lawn of your own home before you could come to any harm."

Mr. Trusnik let out a sigh.

"What are you talking about?"

"I have been alone for too long, I suppose. Having you here—my unwanted guest—you are still a guest. I admit my emotions are getting the best of me, which is never safe for anyone. In this case it appears that I no longer have to actually touch someone. Perhaps it is the house. Did you touch anything I might touch regularly? Never mind. That is impossible to answer."

"You're fucking *rambling*, old man." Kevin thought back to the electrical shock he felt upon taking hold of the knob of the kitchen drawer when he first entered the house. He had attributed the shock to Santa Ana winds, the electrically charged warm winds that blow through the Los Angeles basin. Could the old man be telling the truth?

The old man paced the room, beyond the reach of Kevin and his scalpel. "Those men. The men across the street at your home. They are there in an attempt to keep me from killing you."

"*What?*" Kevin's arm was quite heavy, and he was having trouble holding up his small weapon.

"They are there in an attempt to prevent you from entering my home. You are already here, and they have failed. You are, though it was not your intention upon breaking into my home, already dead and I have already killed you."

Kevin's nose began to bleed, and he wiped at it, then noticed the color of his blood which was the same watery violet he'd noticed earlier.

"What is—what did you—that was not something to make me sleep... What are you?"

"My dear, you seem to have difficulty finishing your sentences," said the large puppet. "Pavel, have you noticed that he seems to have trouble finishing his sentences?"

"My friend there. The large one standing behind you. I call him Cheidu. In his day he was the great stage actor, Robert Lamb. If you studied theatre history or black history in school you might have read a brief paragraph about him. He was also my best friend. And I killed him. It was a tragic accident. He broke so many rules to try to see me and I repaid his kindness and betrayed his friendship by smashing his head open."

Kevin had felt fear when he had been further back in the house, trapped in the snare, tangled in the netting. He had also been annoyed, angry, and indignant that the tables had been so turned upon his plan for the evening, which helped motivate him to get out of the net. This was different. Kevin now knew what it felt like to be terrified.

"Would you believe that you are the first person to come into this house since the year 1950?"

Kevin did not know how to respond. He began figuring out a way to get out of the room and the house. He would call the police once he managed to get out of there. Wait, he could not call the police. They could not know he had been here. The old man was insane, without question. He would have to overtake the man and leave him there.

The old man was a shut-in. If Kevin could take him and get out of the house, no one would know the man was dead for a very long time. Would they? Had someone contacted the old man? How did he know Kevin was coming? And who was searching his house?

"Who is in my house and what do they want?" Kevin asked. Not giving up, his body moving forward by mere centimeters, he moved closer to Mr. Trusnik.

"You have been a very bad person for a very long time now, Kevin, and it is time to put a stop to it."

"You don't know anything."

"I have nothing but time in here to study, to learn, to watch. No, it is not possible for anyone to see in here, but that does not mean that I don't see out and that I have not been here, under house arrest for *decades* without learning everything there is to know about every *living thing* around me. I say *living thing* because it is in my best interest that those *living things* around me stay *living* until the natural order of things determines otherwise. The consequences to me if those *living things* happen to sicken or expire in a way that upsets the natural order of things are quite… grim."

"You're a fucking Peeping Tom, is that what you're saying, you sick fuck?"

"I prefer to refer to myself as the neighborhood watch. A term introduced into the lexicon in the last decade or so. Tell me, Kevin, that garbage bag you carried over to the Hague's house and then dumped the contents on their lawn. Was that their cat, by chance?"

"What? You."

"Yes. I watched you. I saw. You killed your neighbor's cat. For what? Pleasure? A quick thrill? Who here is the 'sick fuck' to use your words?"

Kevin had been moving closer and closer to Trusnik, his hand on the scalpel.

"Is it your intention to attack me with that scalpel you have in your hand?" asked Mr. Trusnik.

Kevin stopped moving. He wiped the blood away from his nose that trickled from one nostril.

"Oh, by all means, keep trying. Don't let me stop you. I have no intention of making my way out of here alive after all of this. It is much too late for that."

"Glad you know what is going to happen," said Kevin.

"Not because of anything brilliant on your part, let me be very clear about that. You are nothing but a psychopath with a limited scope of knowledge and common sense. You're no better than the shark that glides about the ocean without a plan, waiting for the next edible thing to cross its path that it can tear apart and devour."

"Kinda cool to be compared to a shark," said Kevin, trying a different tactic. Maybe if he tried to befriend the man. Maybe agreeing with him. Maybe the old man would let him out.

The old man sighed in exasperation. "Like I said, you're not very bright. Neither is the shark. Sharks are also quite wasteful and leave far too much evidence behind them of their activities. As do you. Those men across the street will find everything they need. And a few things you never thought of. Then they will come here and find you, then me, and will come to certain conclusions, none of which will be that you are the mental genius you think yourself to be."

Kevin decided to try challenging him again. "So what is it? You made this huge claim that 'I'm already dead.' Very dramatic." Kevin inched closer to Mr. Trusnik.

"Did you know I was married once?"

"So? I heard she died."

"Yes. She did."

"Am I supposed to care about that?"

"Perhaps. I killed her."

"You murdered your *wife*?" Kevin asked. He had not expected this. There was nothing in the news, nothing in any of his research on the house or its history, nothing about a woman being murdered.

"Did you go to jail?"

Mr. Trusnik shook his head. Kevin stared in disbelief. Could this man be like him?

"I didn't mean to. It was an avoidable consequence and I should have listened to my advisors. You, on the other hand, are what I refer to as an 'unavoidable consequence.' A home invasion falls under that category."

"How did you kill her?"

"What, you expect something gruesome and sick and twisted? Like something *you* would do?"

"How did you do it?"

Mr. Trusnik walked to the large puppet he referred to as Robert Lamb, reached up and took it down from the mechanism from which it hung. He set it on the bench next to the puppet he had been dancing with when Kevin entered the work room.

"I loved her."

"Yes, yes you said that. How did you kill her?"

"I told you. I loved her."

"That doesn't tell me anything."

Mr. Trusnik began to gather various items together

into a pile. To Kevin's blurred vision, he thought part of it looked like the net he had been caught in. How did the old man get that? He was in the back room the whole time.

"Tell me, Kevin. If you were born with a defect that did not allow you to have any physical contact with others, what would you do?"

"What?" Kevin had not given up on trying to inch closer to the old man, who seemed oblivious to Kevin's movement.

"A simple enough question, but then again I must remember that I am speaking to someone with an even simpler mind. What would you do if you knew that this defect of yours would kill people?"

Kevin stopped. "What, you're some sort of carrier? You have some sort of disease? Is that it? I'm going to catch some disease from you? Don't you have to have a sign on your house, or be in a quarantined hospital somewhere?"

"No. Things do not work that way. Excuse me, I need to check something."

Kevin watched as Mr. Trusnik moved to the ladder, and agile as a squirrel, climbed to the top where a narrow window looked out upon the street. Mr. Trusnik focused his gaze on something outside the window for a moment, moved back down the ladder and to his spot facing Kevin.

"There are more people in your house. They appear to have found something useful. What do you suppose that might be?"

Kevin coughed, and a small bit of violet colored phlegm landed on the front of his shirt. He did not move to wipe it off.

"Or they think I have been kidnapped."

"I take it you watch a lot of television? I assure you, the people across the street are not at your house because they believe you to have been kidnapped."

"How can you know that?"

Mr. Trusnik pulled over a stool and set it in front of Kevin. He sat down.

"I had a call before your arrival. Something about a family. North of here. Quite disturbing news. To think a person could do something like that to an entire family."

"*What?*"

"Yes. That poor family. I'm sure there have been many others. Have there been many others, Kevin?"

A siren was heard coming down the street. Mr. Trusnik looked at Kevin, who returned the look, incredulous. There was no way that this man could know about the last house. No way at all. Yet he did, and there were people searching his home. Other people knew. How many? What would his parents be thinking right now? Where had he left the mp3 player? Top of the dresser, where he always left it. Out in the open. Casual. His parents would never think to listen to anything on it, so he left it out. Shit. *His music.* His beautiful music.

"How?" Kevin asked.

Another siren was heard in the distance. Mr. Trusnik gathered more items into the pile on the workbench.

Mr. Trusnik sighed. "I am what might be considered an important man to some, although they have great reservations about me, with good reason I suppose. There is an organization, a business, that attends to all my affairs, my investments, home improvements, grocery deliveries, et cetera. They also notify me of things that might be of interest to me like, say, someone accessing the blueprint records of my home."

Kevin was surprised. "How long did you know I had the blueprints to your house?"

"Since the day you got them. You were already under a certain amount of scrutiny due to some of your nighttime activities of which I was aware, but you became a subject of extreme interest to quite a large number of people after you took those blueprints. So much for picking a nice old shut-in with no visitors, hmm Kevin?"

Kevin felt that if he could keep talking to the man, he would somehow be okay, that he could escape. "So, why are you so important? What are you, retired CIA or something?"

"You *do* watch a lot of television. *CIA?*"

"Then what are you?"

"Your victims did not deserve what they got from you."

Kevin reached up and grabbed a cloth from off the workbench and put it up to his bleeding nose. He had grown pale, and a blue vein appeared in his forehead and ran from his temple to his cheek.

"You deserve to go to prison for your crimes for the rest of your natural life. You deserve to be beaten and tortured and made to feel terrified every day that you are in prison. I regret to say that what remains of your natural life will not allow that justice."

Kevin peered at the cloth, not comprehending what he was seeing. It was the wrong color for blood, but the flow would not stop. A weird mucus, maybe.

"I do not believe that people should be put to death for their crimes, Kevin. I happen to believe in the more barbaric practice of locking you in an environment with others who are like you and leaving you alone to tear each other apart in your own special way. I think that has more of a ring of justice to it. Capital punishment, the way they have done it all these years, so immediate, so final; a swift and often merciful end to the life of one who was neither swift nor merciful in the treatment of their numerous victims. There is one form of execution that I think would be truly horrible."

"What's that?"

"Being burned alive." Mr. Trusnik had no irony in his voice when he spoke.

"They did that with witches," said Kevin

"And others. Others who were different. Others who, through no fault of their own, were born with something that frightened the majority. An extra finger, a mole, different colored eyes, a pair of wings." Mr. Trusnik moved away from Kevin and over to the pottery kiln, where he adjusted the controls.

Kevin snorted in laughter. "That never happened. So, if you don't believe in the death penalty, what is it that you're doing to me?"

"I don't know."

"What is that supposed to mean? You change up the poison?"

"You are making me repeat myself like a broken record. I told you, you weren't poisoned. The cut you received was from a knife treated with the sap from a root that was to put you to sleep. But you got too far inside the house and touched things that do not belong to you. You got too near me. Do you think a house can take on the emotion of its inhabitants? There is so much grief here. So much sadness. Such loneliness. I am not so old and lacking self-awareness that I do not know what emotions pour out of me day after day, unchecked, for decades. Alone. People need contact with others. Being in solitary confinement from any of it for decades... well, although you are a despicable human being, you are still a human being and I have not been in close contact with one since well before your parents were born."

Kevin felt faint. Clutching the scalpel, he leaned on the bench.

"Kevin, you are getting quite pale, and you should sit down. You may try to get close to me to cut me with your scalpel. You will have to slash my throat when that happens, by the way. It is necessary that I completely bleed out if I am to actually die. One deep cut. Ear to ear should do it."

Even as the old man described the way to kill him, he approached Kevin, reached over and took the scalpel away from him. Kevin was too weak to fight him. He gently carried Kevin to the wall and sat him upon the floor with his back propped against the wall. He then put the scalpel back into Kevin's hand and backed away.

"What are you saying?" asked Kevin, bewildered and disoriented.

"In 1942 I committed a crime. Not the normal kind of crime that you read about in the newspaper or that is even on the law books. But a crime, nonetheless and many people died because of me."

"You killed people?"

"Not like you. Never like you, Kevin. For my sentence, I was given a choice between two things. I chose the more difficult of the two, thinking I deserved some grand and enduring penance because my other choice would have been a swift and humane death, which as I said, I am against."

Mr. Trusnik opened up the pottery kiln and placed objects into the pile he'd collected. The net was one of the things to go in first, followed by the animal snare.

"Did you go to prison?"

"This has been my prison. I have been here since that day. I do not leave, I do not take visitors, though my dear friend visited me once, unannounced, and that did not end well for us. No, I have no contact with the outside world. Everything is delivered. Workmen are dealt with over the phone or Internet. Everything else is handled by the businessmen I told you about."

"1942. That would make you—"

Mr. Trusnik put one finger to the side of his nose. "Exactly. Three hundred years old. This year."

Kevin's eyes followed the old man's movement as he put Kevin's digital recorder into the kiln. In Kevin's weakened state, he chose to listen and did not attempt to respond.

"You are the first human being I have been in close proximity to in seventy years, and I have to say I am feeling quite overwhelmed. My heart is beating rapidly, my pulse is very fast. I am perspiring. I can't remember the last time I did that. I am experiencing some form of passion—I suppose because I actually have a guest? My affliction has always been that harm comes to people when I experience passion. I did not poison you, Kevin. You are dying by being near me."

"Are you going to try to tell me you are some sort of

vampire?"

The old man placed more items in the kiln. One item was similar to the small knife the puppet used to cut him. He turned back to Kevin.

"No. I am not a vampire. You and I both know that vampires are utter nonsense. They make for good novels and movies, however. No. Perhaps my isolation here in this house has made the house like me. I asked before, how many things did you touch when you came in here? When you touched them, did you feel something? Did anything happen?"

Kevin touched his hand, again remembering the tingling sensation in his hand that he shook off as he crept through the kitchen.

Mr. Trusnik mused. "How many items that may have been touched by me? It used to be that I would have to have some form of physical contact with someone to harm them. But that is not true. The others can do it without touching. I remember a small flu epidemic, not started by me. However, it was started *because* of me. I had to know the extent of the damage I'd caused. I asked questions. I found answers. Yes, they touched people, but they also touched *things*, that's how powerful they are. I imagine they envision that alternate outcome for you. I admit I did not think about what might happen to you if you came in here and placed your hands on anything."

"Are you human?"

Mr. Trusnik did not answer, but walked over to the female puppet in the silver-blue lace dress and traced her face with his fingers.

"You've lost blood and what little you have left is

turning to water. I need you to do me one favor before you expire."

Kevin had never been so helpless, so frightened. He stared at the old man, who stared back with an expression that Kevin thought looked almost sad.

"Good. Slow your breathing if you can. It will help. I told you I was under house arrest, and that I was forbidden to come in contact with anyone for the rest of my natural life, which could very well be another hundred years or so. Can you imagine being completely by yourself for that long a period of time?"

Kevin watched Mr. Trusnik. He did not believe half of what he was saying, but believed the old man was convinced it was true. Kevin had no idea what he had been poisoned with, but it was having an effect. He took another wipe at his nose and peered again at the cloth—it looked like clear mucus with a little blood in it. Good. The bloody nose was stopping.

"As I said, Kevin, your blood is becoming water. Or something similar to water."

Did the old man read minds? Kevin said nothing.

"I was told that the punishment for breaking the bonds of my house arrest and having any contact with another human would be that I was to be burned alive. That was *my* choice. My option."

Kevin's speech came in halting efforts, his breathing labored. "Burned alive? No one does that." Kevin eyed the scalpel that lay in his useless hand.

"In my world, they do. As a lesson to others. And I cannot fathom anything more horrible. I admit to having become a coward. I chose this, solitary existence, instead of the sudden death I was offered at my original sentence, because it was not the quick and easy way out that sudden death would bring. I wanted to be punished. And I have been. I don't know why they chose fire to be my punishment if I was ever to have contact with someone again. I stopped trying to figure them out ages ago. So I must ask you to kill me. You were planning to, anyway. This way will not provide you the *music* you were hoping for, but you are here and it is what you came to do. I ask that you do it. Consider it an act of mercy in an attempt at contrition over your many other more heinous acts."

Kevin thought the old man was rambling nonsense, but was in no position from his helpless place on the floor to do anything other than humor him.

"But I broke in. You didn't mean to have contact with me. Can't they do anything, these people of yours? It wasn't your fault."

"Kevin, are you trying to defend me? Or are you trying to save yourself? You can't possibly be trying to find a reason not to kill me."

"I. I don't know. I—" Kevin made one last effort to get to his feet and collapsed back against the wall.

"No. Kevin, I need you for one last thing. I need you to hold on a while longer."

"Mr. Trusnik, I—"

"Oh let us not be formal *now*. That is inappropriate. They will be here soon. The ones that can enter. The ones like me. They will come in here and then they will take me out of my home. They will take me away from my family. They will do this terrible thing. I want to die with my family. At home. You *have* to hold on."

"Your. Family." Oh my God. The old man meant the puppets.

"They will find them. They will know."

Mr. Trusnik walked over to the wire where the puppet of Robert Lamb was attached. He took the puppet down and held him close to his chest, then walked over to the cabinet on the wall and released his close hold on the puppet, placing him inside. "Thank you, Cheidu," he said.

The old man then went back to the workbench where he had placed the skeleton and the waltzing woman puppets he'd used to taunt Kevin in the hallway. Kevin studied them in the light.

"Those look like real skeletons," Kevin said.

"They were my parents," said Mr. Trusnik.

Kevin squinted to see them more clearly. They were indeed skeletons. Kevin could not help but feel a certain fascination for this man.

"When you get to be as old as I am, I don't think some of the same social mores can apply any longer. There is no rule that I am aware of that when a person dies that they *must* be buried or cremated or disposed of in some place. Where better for a puppeteer and his family to be other than immortalized in a puppet theatre? My father referred to me as an escaped puppet who found his way home. He called me that until he died. When my parents died I realized that they too, were puppets that needed to escape and find their way home. I helped them come back. That is all."

Kevin pointed with his head toward the puppet in the dress.

"Then who is the one you were dancing with. Your *wife* or something?"

"Yes. My beautiful Juliet."

"Her name was Juliet?"

"Her name was..." Mr. Trusnik seemed to lose his train of thought. "Wednesday's child is full of woe," he muttered. "Her name was—"

"You don't remember your wife's name? What's wrong with you? Do you have Alzheimer's or something?" Kevin held the cloth to his face.

A knocking sound from deep in the house startled them both.

"I expect they have finished with your home and are here to collect you and take me to wherever it is they take someone with my particular crimes."

"Will they get me to a hospital?" the boy asked.

"I don't think you will make it to the hospital," Mr. Trusnik said. "Is there anything you wish to say? Any regrets? How many people *have* you killed, Kevin?"

Kevin shook his head. Mr. Trusnik nodded. The boy was not going to confess anything to this.

Mr. Trusnik moved toward Kevin. "I think it is time to make you a little more comfortable." He leaned further in toward the wall where Kevin leaned, and Kevin lashed out with the scalpel. Mr. Trusnik took it from Kevin's hand for the second time that evening, and for the second time, Kevin did not have the speed or strength to stop him.

"I'll take that now. You no longer have the strength for what I need." Mr. Trusnik held Kevin's hand for a moment and gave it a pat. Kevin inhaled roughly and looked into Mr. Trusnik's eyes for the first time.

"Your eyes. They are not—"

"Human?" asked Mr. Trusnik. "I think I am far *too*

human and that has been my greatest flaw."

Mr. Trusnik placed the scalpel on the workbench and left the workshop, returning moments later carrying Kevin's duffle bag. He emptied the contents and placed them on the floor around Kevin.

"What are you doing?" Kevin rasped.

"You *did* intrude upon my home with the intention of doing me great harm. You are not an innocent. They will have to know. They must investigate you. Determine your other crimes so that people can have their closure."

"Closure. What is that? Doesn't look like you got any closure. You turned your family into a bunch of freak dolls that you *play* with."

Mr. Trusnik gave Kevin a sad smile.

"I do not expect you to understand the working of my mind any more than I can begin to fathom the workings of yours."

The knocking sounded again. Pavel cocked his head in the direction of the sound.

Kevin gave a feeble chuckle, saying "You gonna answer that?"

It was the last thing Kevin would say. A large volume of clear liquid burst from his nostrils. He inhaled one final, ragged breath, then died.

"So soon," said Pavel, regarding the boy seated on the floor whose eyes were blank, open.

The knocking grew more insistent, and Pavel heard someone trying the knob on the front door. Soon they would go around to the kitchen door and find it unlocked.

Pavel walked over to the puppet made from his wife's bones, and picked her up, placed her back in the cabinet with the puppet of Cheidu. He walked over to the workbench, picked up the scalpel and placed it back in Kevin's hand.

Pavel made a hasty inspection of his home, clearing away evidence of his theatrical show earlier. He placed his parents' puppets back in the cabinet and closed and locked the door. He placed his hand against the closed door of the cabinet. "Goodbye, my dearest escaped puppets. Goodbye."

He picked up the digital sound and light board he created and put it in the pottery kiln with the other objects. He moved with great speed around the areas of the house and workspace where he had items that might be of interest: his computer, his phone book and other items. He placed those in the kiln as well. He adjusted the temperature, closed the kiln and turned it on. Once closed and on the heat cycle it would not unlock again until it was done and cooled down. What didn't melt would be unrecognizable as anything that might be considered evidence when the kiln was opened. He turned on the power, but turned off all lighting, plunging the house into darkness. He turned on the stereo. Mahler's *Ninth Symphony*. How fitting, he thought. The men had reached the back door of the kitchen, and Pavel heard them enter the house.

A voice called, "Pavel Trusnik? Are you all right?" Pavel recognized the voice as McGovern's. He heard the men moving through the house. From the sound of their footsteps they seemed to be looking in every room. They would reach the workshop in a matter of moments. Pavel sat and waited in a chair near the dead body of Kevin.

McGovern and the others entered the room and

carried flashlights and what appeared to be guns. Pavel could see the metal glint of the weapons in the near dark of the room. There seemed to be many more people in his house than he had anticipated.

"Pavel?"

"I'm over here."

McGovern rushed to Pavel's side and shone the flashlight in Pavel's face which caused him to squint and turn his head. "Where are the lights?" McGovern asked.

"On the wall, by the door."

"Get the lights!" McGovern yelled.

The lights came on, and Pavel adjusted his vision. McGovern, Peters, Revera and two others he did not recognize, but knew to be of his own kind, were in the room. They would not endanger human police officers by having them come into this house. Not now.

The men started searching the room. Two split off to search the rest of the house. McGovern looked at Pavel and then over at Kevin, propped against the wall, his supplies placed around him, scalpel in hand.

"It appears that you defended yourself against a violent predator, Pavel. You are lucky to be alive."

"I told you I would handle it."

McGovern seemed to take in the entirety of the workroom in his gaze.

"Something about putting on a show?" he asked.

"Something like that."

"How did he die?" McGovern leaned down to the body and peered at Kevin's skin.

"I did not touch him myself until near the end when it was already too late."

"Where did you touch him?"

"I patted his hand."

McGovern examined the boy's hand. "Patted his hand. I see. And he got to this place at the wall on his own?"

Pavel nodded, lying.

"These things. They are his?"

"Yes. I believe he intended to use them to torture me first, then kill me."

"The scalpel in his hand?"

"His as well. Perhaps your investigators will find evidence of other crimes upon it. He did not strike me as being fastidious. I think the ammonia in the bag was to revive me so he could do more of… whatever it is people like him do."

McGovern stood up from the body.

"I hope there are no other people like him, Pavel."

"What happens now?" asked Pavel. "As if I have to ask."

"I have to meet with the others."

"You were very clear about what would happen if I broke house arrest. People will have to be brought in here. Evidence gathered. People in my home. Attention has been drawn. I know the consequences."

"This house is no longer yours, Pavel. As far as the rest?" McGovern's voice trailed off as one of the men approached the cabinet where Pavel kept his precious puppets, his family.

"I'll need the key that opens this," said the man.

"What is your name?" asked Pavel.

"Dunnegan." He was a large man, similar in size to McGovern. Another man who could, like McGovern, pass for someone in law enforcement, a detective of some kind.

"Alright, Dunnegan. Give me a moment." Pavel moved to rise from his chair and stumbled, landing on the floor near Kevin's body. McGovern helped him to his feet.

"Before you open that, do you think it would be all right if I went out to my garden? One last time. I wish to breathe the night air in my own garden before I have to leave here."

Dunnegan was insistent. "I need you to let me open this."

"Of course. The key is a little tricky." He took the key from around his neck. "May I go outside?"

McGovern took the key from Pavel, who then let himself out the door into the back yard garden. McGovern opened the drapes so he could watch him as he stood there.

Dunnegan unlocked the cabinet and inspected the interior. He stared at the contents for a minute, not comprehending. "McGovern? Can you take a look at this?"

McGovern joined Dunnegan and looked inside the cabinet. Realization came to him, along with sudden nausea.

"We'll need to take these with us," McGovern said. "Carefully. Carefully!" He fought the urge to retch.

"What are they?" asked Dunnegan.

"The remains of his parents, his wife and our missing Robert Lamb," said McGovern.

Dunnegan looked back in the cabinet, took a small screwdriver from off the work table and used it to lift the fabric of the dress on the puppet that had, in life, been Žophie. He saw the skeleton underneath the fabric, immediately dropped his hand and the tool and backed away from the cabinet.

"My God," he said.

McGovern gazed out the window at the old man standing in the light from the street lamps and the moon. There was something unusual about his posture, and McGovern's eyes quickly scanned Kevin's body for the scalpel. It was gone.

"Damn him! Get outside, now!" They rushed to the door, but the latch had been pulled so the door was locked. When the men finally broke through, McGovern was first outside. He ran to Pavel who had sunk to his knees. Blood rushed from his throat where he had cut himself from ear to ear with the scalpel.

"Pavel, no. You did not have to do this," McGovern said, anguished.

Pavel could no longer speak, for blood rushed from the wound which he'd made with a deep cut, thoroughly, finally. He reached up to McGovern with both arms, a last attempt at an embrace with another.

McGovern knelt next to Pavel Trusnik, took him in his arms, and held him.

The End.

Acknowledgments

I like to think that writing is a solitary art form, best done while wearing my bathrobe with a full cup of coffee at the ready, dogs breathing softly at my feet. The truth is, however, that many people were involved in the final product that is this little yarn.

First and foremost, I wish to thank my friends and family for their unconditional support, particularly my husband for convincing me to finish what began as a short story that I had stopped writing. He wanted to know how it ended. To my parents, George and Avon Wilson, for being such good cheerleaders, enthusiastic readers and gobblers of all forms of fiction and for their bravery when reading this story in its roughest state. I wish to thank my friend Bryan Bellomo for also braving that early draft. A forever thank you goes to my sister, Alena, for that life-changing and crucial sister-talk that gave me the courage to give myself permission to write. I miss you every day.

I would like to express tremendous gratitude to my editor, Becky Eagleton. This book would not be readable without her keen eye and red pen.

I shout out my profound love to every sound, set, lighting and technical director I have ever had the privilege to work with during my 30 years in live theatre. You are golden geniuses. Again, I thank my husband, this time for his vast knowledge of all things Civil War, hence my discovery of the actual and horrific events of Fort Pillow. I thank my dear friend John McGehee for sharing his knowledge of 18th century plumbing that led to further information on cholera epidemics (such a cheery subject). I thank the expertise of my father, George Paul Wilson, PhD., Acoustical & Vibration Consultant for Wilson, Ihrig & Associates, Inc. for technical advice on how to construct a multi-directional sound system. My wholehearted appreciation and thanks go to my 'marionette consultant,' the tremendously talented Douglas Strich, Puppet Builder for the New York City Parks Foundation. His generous and patient answers to my questions about how those amazing creatures come to life was like getting a chest full of treasure. If I have made any errors, they are strictly mine.

Thank you to my writing mentor Che'Rae Adams, the Los Angeles Writers Center, and the online fellowship of IWU for letting me troll through your freely given support and information. Lastly, I'd like to thank my friend and fellow author, Christine DeMaio-Rice, for introducing me to this crazy new world and guiding me through the process. You are, to use your words, simply sausage.

About the Author

Alisa Tangredi came to the world of writing later in life, following a 30-year career as an actress in theatre, with sporadic employment in commercials and television. Under the name Alisa Wilson, she has written a few short stories and several plays, both full-length and one-act, including: *Art Is Useless When You're Being Mauled By a Bear*, *Canis Major*, *Laehmly Park*, *Confidence*, and *The Bay of Smokes*, co-written with her sister, the late Alena Kathleen Wilson, for the first annual L.A. History Project (performed at LATC). *The Puppet Maker's Bones* is her first novel. She lives in Lake Balboa, California, with her husband, Bart, and their two dogs.

Made in the USA
Charleston, SC
21 September 2012